SEBASTIAN'S GOLD

SEBASTIAN'S GOLD

A TREASURE HUNT THROUGH PORTUGAL'S AZORES ISLANDS

R.D.D. SMITH

Modelbenders Press

Sebastian's Gold: A Treasure Hunt Through Portugal's Azores Islands

© Copyright 2024 by Roger D. Smith. All rights reserved. No part of this book may be reproduced or transmitted in any form or by any means, electronic or mechanical, including photocopying, recording, or by any information storage and retrieval system, without written permission from the author. Find out more at **http://www.rddsmith.com/**

AI Disclaimer: All the text, characters, and plot were created by a human author. Therefore, it is all covered by copyright. AI contributions are described in the "AI Disclosure" section at the end.

Modelbenders Press books may be purchased for business and promotional use. For more information, please contact the publisher. Inquire with the author at **http://www.rddsmith.com/**

PRINTED IN THE UNITED STATES OF AMERICA

Interior and Cover Designed by Adina Cucicov at Flamingo Designs

The Library of Congress has cataloged the paperback edition:

Smith, R.D.D.
Sebastian's Gold: A Treasure Hunt Through Portugal's Azores Islands
/ R.D.D. Smith–1st ed.
1. Action Adventure, 2. Travelogue, 3. Thriller
I. R.D.D. Smith   II. Title.

Paperback ISBN 978-1-938590-40-5
Hardback ISBN 978-1-938590-41-2
eBook ISBN 978-1-938590-39-9

FICTION BY R.D.D. SMITH

Dr. Monica Gray, Medical Thriller Series
The Surgeon in the Mirror
Against a Viral Threat
Savior of the War Torn

Short Stories
The Surgeon's Genie
Freyja $AI
Jack Hunter: One More Mission

Global Runners Travelogue Series
Blood on the Equator
Sebastian's Gold

NONFICTION BY ROGER D. SMITH

Chief Technology Officer
Thinking About Innovation
In the Footsteps of Franklin
Advice Written on the Back of a Business Card

Join our community of readers to receive fascinating news, speculative fiction, and discussions related to the novels. www.rddsmith.com/free

TABLE OF CONTENTS

CHAPTER 1

ALONE

Lauren Banister sat alone at a table at an outdoor café in Lisbon's Alfama district, where cobblestone streets wound like ancient serpents through the city's oldest quarter. The wrought-iron table's surface was entirely covered by her maps and notebooks, as well as a forgotten cup of coffee growing cold as she concentrated. Her long, brown hair hung to each side of her face, creating a cave of solitude within which she could work, a habit she'd developed during long hours in university libraries.

The cacophony of tourist chatter, the calls of vendors, and the distant clang of the famous yellow trams barely penetrated her focus. At thirty-two, Lauren had mastered the art of creating her own bubble of concentration anywhere in the world. Her weathered hiking boots, crossed and tucked beneath the table, contrasted with her otherwise professional appearance—a concession to the dual nature of her work as both an academic and a field researcher.

São Miguel. The name seemed to pulse on the map before her. One of the earliest of the Azores Islands visited by sailors and pirates, its volcanic peaks were shrouded in mystery and legend. *The perfect place to hide a treasure*, she thought, running a finger along its coastline. Her archaeologist's mind was already busily cataloging potential sites, calculating access paths, and analyzing historical patterns.

She reached for her coffee, grimacing at its coldness when it passed her lips, and caught her reflection in the café window. Hazel eyes, tanned face, and a small scar above her right eyebrow—a souvenir from her first dig in Mexico—stared back at her. Ten years of fieldwork had left their mark, but she wouldn't have it any other way.

Lauren leafed through her leather-bound notebook, its pages filled with her precise handwriting documenting facts and legends collected over months of research. For centuries, pirates, Navies, and even kings had considered these islands magical stepping stones between worlds. She'd documented dozens of legends of hidden treasures and lost fortunes thus far. If even one proved true…

That thought triggered another: *I won't let history repeat itself.* Her jaw tightened as memories of Victor surfaced unbidden in her mind. He'd been brilliant, a talented geologist with charm and vision that had swept her off her feet. They'd shared everything: research, adventures, their bed, their dreams — until that day in Israel when they'd finally discovered something extraordinary. His betrayal still burned three years later. He had left without so much as a goodbye, and he had taken with him the artifacts they'd uncovered together.

Never again, she thought. With an angry shake of her head, Lauren forced her attention back to the map before her. Red ink marked her careful annotations, identifying likely landing sites from the Age of Discovery, caves mentioned in sailors' journals, and locations where old coins had surfaced over the centuries. Many of these clues surrounded the dormant volcano dominating São Miguel's landscape.

If something is hidden here, it's in that volcano, Lauren thought, her analytical mind already calculating angles and approaches. *But where exactly?* The map showed several possibilities, each with its own historical significance.

She'd come to Lisbon hoping to find answers in a legendary antiquities shop. Rumors circulating among her academic peers spoke of an elderly owner who knew the secrets of countless historical treasures. Three days of searching the twisted streets had yielded her nothing but frustration. The shop seemed as mythical as the treasures she sought.

Lauren began gathering her materials, carefully folding the maps and tucking them into her enormous backpack. She would have to proceed to the islands without whatever secrets this mysterious shopkeeper might have possessed. But that was fine—she'd always done her best work alone. At least when she was alone, she could trust her instincts without second-guessing someone else's motives.

Standing up, she dropped a few euros on the table and shouldered her bag. The late afternoon sun cast long shadows through the narrow streets, and a cool breeze carried the salty scent of the nearby Atlantic. Tomorrow, she would board a small plane to São Miguel. Whatever secrets the volcanic island held, Lauren was determined to uncover them—on her own terms this time.

Her boots clicked against the ancient cobblestones as she walked away from the café, her mind already racing ahead to consider the challenges that awaited her in the Azores. She'd learned from her mistakes. This time would be different. This time, she would find what she was looking for, and no one would take it from her.

ANTIQUITIES AND ALLEYWAYS

John and Sandra Crisman wandered excitedly through the back streets of Lisbon. They were a few days early for their organized vacation group.

The streets twisted and turned like a labyrinth, each corner revealing a new facet of the city's ancient character. Cobblestones, worn smooth by centuries of footsteps, glistened under the autumn sun. Colorful tiles adorned the facades of buildings, their intricate patterns telling stories of bygone eras. The aroma of freshly baked pastries mingled with the earthy breeze from the nearby Tagus River, creating an intoxicating blend that was uniquely Lisbon. Street vendors called out in melodic Portuguese, offering everything from fragrant spices to handcrafted trinkets, while the distant tunes of Fado music added a soulful soundtrack to their exploration.

"It has to be close. My friend said it was definitely on this street," John assured his wife as he turned onto another narrow street. Muttering to himself, he said, "Turn right immediately past the café with the blue and white awning. Then, in another hundred feet, look for the marking on the wall."

"Is it the same friend who sent us into the red-light district of Amsterdam looking for lost letters from Anne Frank?"

"No. I told you, that guy was a charlatan. This new guy is the real deal. He knows where to find rare artifacts."

Sandra thought, *Sure, he does.* But just like every other journey she had joined her husband on, she kept her suspicions to herself. Sometimes, these trips worked out. More frequently, there was nothing to be found at the end of the rainbow. To be fair, though, it was always an adventure.

John and Sandra, a Floridian couple in their mid-fifties with a shared passion for traveling, complemented each other well. John, with his sun-weathered skin and perpetually curious eyes, approached treasure hunting with the enthusiasm of a child. Sandra, his steadfast partner, balanced his impulsive nature with her thoughtful pragmatism. Together, they had turned treasure hunting into a side hobby during their travels, seeking the stories hidden within the artifacts rather than just their monetary gain. The married couple's shared experiences had woven a rich tapestry of memories, each new quest adding another vibrant thread.

"There! That's it!" John looked at the picture on his phone and compared it to the symbol on the side of the building. "We're supposed to go through the door to the right of that symbol."

Sandra looked at the illustration. It appeared to form a human fist. "So, we spent all this time looking for a boxing gym?"

"No, it's a symbol of good luck or protection."

"What if that door goes into someone's home?"

"It doesn't. It's an antiquities shop, I promise."

Pushing the door open, the couple stepped into the past. The shop was a treasure trove in itself, a dimly lit sanctuary filled with relics from different eras. Scanning the room, Sandra felt as though they had traveled back a hundred years. The tables, wall coverings, and lights all looked like they hadn't been changed in over a century.

Shelves bowed under the weight of dusty tomes, ancient maps, and ornate trinkets. The air was thick with the scent of aged wood and leather, mingling with the faint aroma of incense. Intricately woven rugs covered the floor, their colors muted by time. Each item seemed to whisper secrets of its past, waiting for the right person to unlock its story. The soft glow of amber lamps cast warm pools of light, accentuating the room's rich textures and inviting visitors to explore.

An old man looked up from his desk in the back. It was cluttered with small, brass parts. He appeared to be repairing a small machine, maybe a clock or an ornate lock. The owner didn't rise as one would expect in America. He swiveled his chair in their direction and opened his arms wide. "*Bem-vindo à minha cidade das maravilhas,*" he said in a hoarse voice. It was weak, but still full of enthusiasm.

John moved closer to him. "Excuse me? We're Americans. English?"

The old man nodded and repeated the greeting. "Of course. Welcome to my city of wonders!"

"Thank you. It's an amazing place."

"It has been amazing for almost 300 years. My father and all the fathers in my family have been in this same place." He pointed to a large wooden plaque above his head. It was a solid piece with a pyramid of faces carved into its surface. Beneath each face was a single word and a number—a name and a year. John and Sandra both stared at it, taking in its age and meaning. It was a family tree showing the owners of this shop. It started with "Emilio, 1752." As their eyes scanned down the plaque, they could see the seams where new pieces of wood had been added to continue the tree. At the bottom was the name Emilio again and the year 1972. Below "Emilio, 1972," there was open space for the generations that would follow.

The room was completely silent while the Americans scanned the tree of proprietors. This history assured John that his friend had been correct. Here was a legitimate purveyor of antiquities. It was not a tourist shop selling trinkets made in China and disguised as local artisanry.

John broke the silence first. "I'm astounded by the history and the beauty of your shop. There are so few like it in the world."

"Yes, that is true. There are none like it anywhere in Lisbon," Emilio stated in a matter-of-fact way. "Are you looking for something specific?"

"I am. I've heard of ancient coins that were minted with the sign of the *figa* on them. The legend says that King Sebastian had them struck before joining the battle in Morocco."

"Of course, I am familiar with this legend. Our Lost King disappeared at the Battle of Alcácer Quibir, the

Battle of the Three Kings, in 1578. We await his return when Portugal needs him the most."

John knew this history as well. The local Sebastianism movement had kept the hope of the returning king alive for nearly 500 years. For decades after his disappearance, the country hoped that the king would literally return in the flesh. But as that hope eroded, Sebastian became a symbol of the prosperous times in Portugal. Today, Sebastianism was a symbol for influential leaders who would bring Portugal into prosperity.

John also knew the part of the legend that claimed, before his departure, Sebastian had struck thousands of gold coins with the talisman of the *figa* and ordered them hidden until his return. He feared that, in his absence, a foreign army would overrun Lisbon and carry away its treasures. He also suspected that the government he left behind would spend or embezzle the country into poverty if they had access to all its gold. The hidden treasure was meant to preserve the country's wealth until Sebastian's return.

Emilio continued, "You seek the hidden royal treasure of *figa* coins. You are not the first. Treasure hunters have searched for 500 years. In all that time, only a dozen of the coins have been discovered, each in a different part of the country. Why do you think you can do better?"

John tipped his head in a sign of humility. "*Senhor* Emilio, I am not a treasure hunter in the traditional sense.

I'm more interested in following history. During my brief visit to your country, I want to follow in the footsteps of this great legend. I don't expect to find treasure. I hope to feel the excitement, the urgency, the sense of mission that your forefathers had. It is a way to taste the richness of Portugal's history."

Emilio remained silent. He had entertained dozens of treasure hunters in this very shop in his half-century as its owner. Some were looking to purchase the *figa* gold if they could find it. Others sought to discover an ancient map. The most extreme were looking for the bones or preserved body of King Sebastian in some lost cave. But a seeker of the country's history was a rare, yet welcome, sight.

CHAPTER 3

TWO SIDES OF THE COIN

"**S**enhor American, you are on a different quest. I have some things to show you." Emilio reached into his pocket and extracted a singular, small object. He placed it on the counter where John and Sandra could see it.

The coin glinted softly in the dim light, its golden hue subdued, yet undeniably rich. Time had smoothed its face and edges, lending it an aura of ancient mystery. Each touch had burnished its surface, telling tales of countless hands that had held it before.

John's mouth hung open, and Sandra gasped at the sight.

"Can I touch it?" John asked.

"Certainly. It has been handled for hundreds of years. It won't break now."

John pinched the coin by its outer edge and raised it to his eyes. On the face, he could make out the image of a fist with the thumb tucked between the index and middle fingers. It was the *figa* sign, which warded off evil spirits and brought good fortune. This coin confirmed the ancient rumors about King Sebastian minting these coins before setting off to war. John had heard the stories, of course, but he had never seen pictures or proof of their existence.

"This coin is amazing. It is just as the legend describes," John whispered to himself. Turning the coin over, he saw a crown on the backside. As it turned, there was a twinkle of light reflected off the image of the crown. It was so quick and bright that he blinked his eyes and glanced up to see where the light had come from. There was no beam coming through a window. He glanced at Sandra to see her reaction to the flash, but her face showed no trace of surprise. Looking back at the coin, its surface was the same rich, dull gleam of gold that he saw on the other side. The reflection was gone.

The crown was an intriguing design, with nine distinct points forming a regal silhouette. Its edges had been softened by time, yet the craftsmanship remained clear. Unlike modern coins, this one bore no inscriptions, no dates, nothing but the *figa* and the crown, as if simplicity itself was part of its magic.

Returning his attention to the owner, John asked, "Where did it come from?"

"My father's, father's, father found it more than a century ago. It was in the 1800s sometime, but the exact year has been forgotten." Pointing to the family tree over his head, he added, "Diego found it in the craggy cliffs along the coast when he was a boy. He brought it home to his father. The family has kept it as a talisman of good luck. It has protected us from evil and guided our fortunes for generations."

Sandra spoke for the first time since entering the store. "If your family found this one coin, then the legends telling of thousands of them could be true."

Emilio nodded. "The legend is definitely true. There are more, but only a few have ever been found. The families who have them keep them well-guarded. The good fortune they bring is worth more than any price the market could offer."

John asked, "Why are you showing it to me? I'm a stranger."

"Because you are not looking for the treasure. You are seeking adventure. I wanted you to know that your quest was not just for ghosts. But you should also know that the quest could be dangerous. Others have dedicated their lives to finding this treasure. To them, it is a serious mission. Do not trust them."

"Thank you. We will be careful. Where should we start?" John asked.

Emilio motioned for the couple to follow him to the back of the shop. In the corner, he pointed to an ancient framed map on the wall.

The map was a masterpiece of cartography, its parchment faded to a sepia tone with age. Intricate lines traced the contours of the coastline, while tiny illustrations of sea creatures and ships adorned the open waters. The map seemed alive, as if it held the pulse of history itself.

"This map was drawn in the 1600s. It is said to have been copied from one that was made for King Sebastian in 1578 before he departed." Pointing to a small city on the coast, he said, "This spot is ancient Lisbon. Treasure hunters all begin here. Some go inland, and others go to sea. None have been successful so far. So, no one knows who is right."

John suggested, "But your ancestor found that coin on the rocky shores along the ocean?"

Emilio smiled and raised his eyebrows. He otherwise didn't reply.

Encouraged, John continued, "So, we will look to the sea. Our vacation was headed in that direction, anyway. We have a few days before we rendezvous with our Global Runners Travel group in the Azores." Then, looking at Emilio, he asked, "Which of the islands would you go to?"

"The island most frequently mentioned in ancient legends is São Miguel. I would look there first."

Turning to his wife for confirmation, John hoped she was game. Sandra spoke firmly, "Then that is where we shall go."

Emilio inclined his head. "I hope you enjoy your quest. Be sure to notice the beauty of my country and our island cousins along the way. Those will be your most precious reward. You are unlikely to see the gold coins that have eluded treasure hunters for 500 years."

"That is wise advice, *senhor*. We appreciate your trust and encouragement."

Sandra spoke next as the two exited the store and wandered back onto the street. "Honey, I think we need to book tickets to São Miguel Island."

DARK PLANS

Its faded, blue exterior barely visible in the gathering dusk, the Bar Atlântico sat like a weathered sentinel on the harbor front of Ponta Delgada. Inside, Duarte Escobar occupied his usual corner booth, where shadows gathered thick as cigarette smoke. At sixty-two, his face was a topographical map of hard years, each wrinkle earned through decades of controlling the underground economy of the Azores.

Victor Rivera spotted him immediately. The geologist had done his homework—Escobar might have dressed like a simple fisherman, but his influence reached all the way from the docks to government offices. Everyone Victor had questioned had pointed him here, their voices dropping to whispers at the mention of Escobar's name.

"*Senhor* Escobar?" Victor approached, using the honorific he'd been told to use. His own appearance was carefully cultivated: successful American, but one capable of rough field work.

"*Si.*" The word emerged like gravel under tires, Escobar's lips barely moving beneath his salt-and-pepper mustache. His dark eyes, sharp as obsidian, measured the American standing before him.

"I'm Victor Rivera. I understand you're the man to consult before undertaking any…significant ventures in the Azores."

Escobar's weathered hand gestured to the empty chair in front of him. "Sit." He lifted his glass of vinho verde, studying Victor over its rim. "Tell me why you're here."

Victor placed his briefcase on the table, keeping his movements deliberate and respectful. "I'm a geologist by training. I specialize in finding things that others have lost." He paused, choosing his next words carefully. "Three years ago, I located a significant cache of scrolls in Israel. The academic community was quite impressed."

"Ah, yes." Escobar's mouth curved slightly. "I read about this discovery. Was there not some controversy? A female colleague who claimed…"

"Lauren Banister," Victor cut in, his jaw tightening at her name. "My former partner. She became unstable when success was within reach. She made wild accusations against me."

"And yet, you prevailed."

"The artifacts spoke for themselves." Victor's smile didn't reach his eyes. "I've learned a lot since then. Solo ventures are risky. Local partnerships are essential."

Escobar leaned forward, his voice dropping when he asked, "And what brings you to my islands?"

Victor extracted a folder from his briefcase. "I've spent six months researching historical records and geological surveys. I believe there's something significant hidden here. Something that would interest collectors who don't ask too many questions about provenance."

"Many treasure hunters come to these islands," Escobar said dismissively. "They find nothing but volcanic rock and empty caves."

"They don't have my expertise. Or my resources." Victor spread out several maps marked with precise annotations. "Or my motivation."

"And what is your motivation, *Senhor* Rivera?"

Victor's facade cracked slightly. "Redemption. Lauren's here, too. She's been asking questions in Lisbon. I think she's onto something new."

Escobar studied him for a long moment. "So, this is personal. Good. Personal motivation makes men careful." He gestured to the maps. "Continue."

For the next hour, Victor outlined his plan. Escobar asked pointed questions about logistics, timing, and potential complications. His questions revealed an intimate knowledge of the islands' geography and the habits of local authorities.

Finally, Escobar sat back. "You will need accommodations, transportation, equipment. These things are simple. But moving certain items off the islands without official attention — this task requires delicate handling. *My* handling."

"That's why I'm here."

"Fifty percent," Escobar stated flatly. "Non-negotiable. And I personally oversee the operation. My men are good for simple tasks, but this one requires…discretion."

Victor flinched at the figure, but he knew he had to accept. "Agreed." He extended his hand for a handshake.

Escobar ignored it. "One more thing. Your former partner — if she becomes a problem?"

"She won't," Victor said quickly. Too quickly.

"Good." Escobar finally shook Victor's hand, his grip surprisingly strong. "Welcome to the Azores, *Senhor* Rivera. Tomorrow, we begin."

As Victor gathered his materials, Escobar watched him with the patient eyes of a predator. He'd seen men like this American before—ambitious, ruthless, carrying wounds that drove them to dangerous decisions. Such men were useful until they weren't.

CHAPTER 5

THE CLOISTER

Staring out of the airplane windows, John said, "There's nothing but ocean out here. It's like we're headed back to the United States."

From the air, São Miguel Island suddenly emerged like an emerald jewel set in the vast blue of the Atlantic Ocean. Lush, green forests blanketed its rolling hills, and the volcanic peaks rose majestically above the landscape. Crystalline lakes nestled within ancient craters shimmered in the sunlight, creating a patchwork of blues and greens. The island's coastline was rugged and dramatic, with cliffs plunging into the sea and small villages dotting the shores.

"Look, there are two islands. They look like a pair of knees sticking up from a giant bathtub." Sandra held her head against the window and pointed forward. "Oh, they're covered in green forest, and I can see a lake in the middle of one. I think that's São Miguel. Just the place to hide a treasure."

John leaned in to get a better look.

From across the aisle, they heard a young woman's voice say, "You're Americans headed to the Azores for vacation?"

Both of them turned to see the face of a young brunette smiling in their direction. Sandra nodded. "Yes, we're doing a little exploring on our own before meeting our travel guides."

"Really? Me, too. My group doesn't get together until Saturday, but I wanted to see a little more of Portugal on my own." She extended her hand across the aisle. "I'm Lauren Banister. From Baltimore."

"I'm John. This is my wife, Sandra. We flew over from Florida."

"So, you're used to the heat and humidity, then." Lauren tried to see the islands through the Sandra's window. "I'm planning to hike that volcano."

"We might do something like that later, but first, we want to dig into the history of the island."

The pilot interrupted their conversation with announcements about landing. All three settled into their seats and performed the universal landing rituals.

Later, while standing at baggage claim, Sandra checked her phone for a signal. John scanned the conveyer belt for their luggage.

Lauren Banister reappeared and snatched a huge hiking backpack from the belt. "Hey, there's mine." Then, turning to the older couple, she said, "I hope you have a wonderful time. I've got to run to catch my driver. We're headed up the volcano right away. Maybe we'll run into each other again." She waved before disappearing.

"She's such a nice girl. I wonder if she's hiking out there alone?" Sandra asked.

"Certainly looked like she was on a solo trip," John conceded while hoisting a bag from the belt.

"Welcome to São Miguel," the driver greeted them when they exited the airport. "Of course, we are named for the archangel you call Saint Michael. He has appeared to our people on the island and the mainland many times over the centuries. He watches over us and ensures our safety and tranquility."

"You certainly need it with the frequent volcanic eruptions," Sandra quipped.

"Yes, and we are always kept safe from the devil's attempts to chase us off the island."

The banter continued as they proceeded to the hotel accommodations.

"You're very lucky to have found rooms at the Convento de São Francisco. It is highly coveted," the driver said as he pulled up to the front of the facility.

The Convento de São Francisco stood as a testament to the island's rich history. Built in the 17th century, its stone walls were weathered by time, yet it exuded an air of quiet dignity. The convent's architecture blended Gothic and Baroque styles, with arched windows and a serene courtyard filled with fragrant flowers. Inside, the walls were lined with ancient tapestries and religious relics, whispering stories of the nuns who once walked these corridors.

"Very lucky. It was the last room available," John conceded. He didn't mention the premium price he'd paid to secure the room on such short notice.

After they had settled into the restored but rustic room, Sandra asked, "Shall we begin our exploration?"

"Sure. Emilio suggested we would find clues here about Sebastian's treasure."

"As paying guests, we have the run of most of the compound. There may be a few places where we have to tiptoe quietly and hope not to get caught." Towards the end of the sentence, her voice pitched higher in anticipation. Sandra was always the one eager to slip behind the "off-limits" signs.

Together, they walked across the ancient courtyards. Visited the restored nuns' quarters. Tiptoed through the chapel. Stumbled into the administrative offices. No one interrupted their poking and prodding.

John pointed to a giant tapestry on the wall in the offices. "Honey, look at this. It's a map of the islands, similar to the one we saw in Emilio's shop. But look, the islands are all in the wrong places."

"Yes, I see that." Sandra thought for a minute. "I'll bet this one was created before modern navigation. Sailors drew what they measured, but the distances from one island to the next were large enough that they lost track. Or maybe they just arrived at a different island than the one they were aiming for, like Christopher Columbus did."

"So, this map is what the world looked like when Sebastian was hiding his treasure? He would have been working with a map that wasn't accurate?"

"I think so. He was hiding the gold in the 1500s. So, if this map was the accepted picture from that time, it would have been what he used as a reference."

"Notice that the only features on São Miguel are the volcano and the lakes inside it. They thought it covered the entire island."

Sandra pointed to a shape on the inner wall of the volcano. "On the side of the caldera, that looks like a pool or spring with a stream running down it." She tipped her head sideways to see it better, and that was when she noticed something amazing. "John, what do you see when you tip your head?"

John followed her example, and the shape jumped out at him. "It's a *figa* symbol!" A broad smile cracked his face. "We should get our hiking boots on."

CHAPTER 6

BLUE-EYED PRINCESS

Sandra stood on the shore of the Lagoon of Seven Cities. She could see the deep blue water in front of her, but this lake had two distinct halves. It was divided by a land bridge, and the other half was a murky, green color in stark contrast to the piece in front of her. It was her turn to show off her knowledge of the island. "John, you know that it's really two very different lakes that sit side-by-side, not one big body of water, right? This half is full of cool water from the surrounding mountains. The other half receives the runoff from several hot springs. It's warmer and full of sediment, which algae thrives on. So, it's a murky green. We'll be able to see both halves clearly once we hike up the side of the volcano."

John replied, "So, what are we waiting for? Let's check out some of those hot springs that feed into the green side of the lake."

The pair set off on the well-marked trail to the King's Viewpoint. Their plan was to hop off that trail and into the jungle to find the hot springs. As they climbed, the two halves of the lake came into clear view. The contrast in colors was striking from their higher vantage point.

Sandra continued listing off more facts that she had learned, "According to legend, the two lakes were formed by the tears of a blue-eyed princess who was separated from her green-eyed shepherd lover by her father, the king. Obviously, the king didn't want his daughter marrying beneath her station. So, together, the pair cried the tears that formed the lakes."

"And that legend would have attracted the attention of King Sebastian centuries later when he sought a place to hide his treasure," John added.

"Perhaps," Sandra agreed.

As they continued their hike, the trail wound through dense vegetation, and the scent of earth and foliage enveloped them. Birds flitted between branches, their calls echoing through the trees. Creating intricate patterns on the ground, the sunlight dappled the path. The air was alive with the sounds of nature, a symphony of rustling leaves and distant waterfalls.

After an hour, John asked, "Do you smell that?" He sniffed at the air and crinkled his nose at the offending scent.

Sandra answered, "Sulfur. There's a spring near here. The breeze is coming from that direction." She pointed to the left of the trail.

They continued up the established trail, and within a quarter mile, John spotted trampled vegetation in the direction they wanted to go. "Shall we?"

"After you, Dr. Livingston," Sandra joked.

They stomped and stumbled along the half-formed trail they'd discovered. It ran parallel to the inner wall of the volcano, neither climbing nor descending. The smell of sulfur grew stronger, suggesting that they were headed in the right direction.

John stopped and held up his hand. "Shhh. I think I hear someone."

Both stood completely still, listening for signs of life.

Sandra whispered, "It sounds like cursing to me."

John nodded. "Let's get a little closer."

Soon, they could make out words. Sandra said, "It's a woman's voice. Speaking English, not Portuguese. I think she said something about 'this damned map,' but I'm not sure."

As they stood silently, the source of the cursing stepped through the foliage right in front of them.

"Aieee!" the woman screamed.

"Gaahaa!" John responded.

Also surprised, but still in control of her emotions, Sandra shouted, "Lauren?"

As everyone recovered from their unexpected encounter, expressions of recognition lit up their faces.

Lauren said, "You're the American couple from the airplane."

John said, "Yes, right. That's right. John and Sandra Crisman. From Florida." Then, he added, "I'm so sorry we scared you. We didn't expect to see anyone out here."

Lauren responded, "No, neither did I. Obviously."

Sandra asked, "What are you doing in the middle of the jungle alone?"

Lauren looked nervously at the couple and began folding the map in her hands. "Umm, going on an adventure, like I said at the airport. I'm looking for the hot springs that feed into the lake. They say it was a popular spot for sailors who landed here. I thought if I was lucky, I'd find an artifact or something."

Pointing at the object in her hands, John asked, "And you have a map of the location?"

"Well, I made a map. I collected details from the stories I'd heard and marked up my own map, but I still can't find the spring. I can smell it, all right, but it's not on this well-established trail here." She waved mockingly at the tiny path they stood on. "And when I venture off the trail, I can't find anything at all." Then she looked back at the couple. "What are *you* doing in the middle of the jungle?"

Sandra sighed. "You might call us amateur treasure hunters. When we hear about a lost temple, treasure, statue, or document, we go looking for it. It's just a fun hobby for us, though. We rarely find anything. It just makes our vacations more interesting."

Lauren's eyes narrowed. "Treasure? What treasure?"

With that question, John launched into an explanation of King Sebastian's *figa* treasure. When he finished, he added, "And, just like you, I thought the soldiers hiding a treasure might think the springs feeding the lake were a good place to hide the gold and retrieve it later."

"Is this treasure real? Or just a legend?" Lauren asked innocently.

John shrugged. "It doesn't matter. It just has to be an adventure for us to enjoy."

Lauren said, "Well, I've clearly failed to find these springs. So, would you mind if I tag along with you? Maybe you'll have better luck."

Sandra smiled. "Yes, that would be splendid. Please, join us."

Looking in the direction that Lauren had emerged from the jungle, John turned and headed off the trail in the opposite direction. Repeatedly, he raised his face and sniffed at the air.

Sandra and Lauren talked occasionally as their quest led them down the mountain slope. John was too immersed in navigating with his nose held high in the air.

CHAPTER 7

STONE *FIGA*

The caldera was a hidden paradise, a lush tapestry of tropical vegetation sprawling over ancient volcanic rock. Ferns and wildflowers clung to every surface, and vines draped from twisted trees, creating a canopy that filtered the sunlight into a soft, dappled glow. Alive with the gentle hum of insects and the distant call of exotic birds, the air was humid and fragrant with the scent of earth and blooming plants.

The two women continued talking while they looked around. "Lauren, what is this tour group you're meeting up with?"

"Oh, it's a small company. They organize trips for runners around the world."

"Wait! Is it Global Runners Travel?"

Lauren's face filled with surprise. "Yes, how do you know them?"

"We're on the same trip. We came early for a little treasure hunting. Then we have to fly to Faial on Saturday to join up with the entire group."

"Me, too! What a crazy coincidence! I'll bet we're on the same flight."

John interrupted the pair. "There it is." He pointed through the foliage at a small pool of water. The sulfur smell was distinctly rising from it. A stream trickled out of the edge and continued down the slope toward the massive green lake.

"Good job, honey. That's quite a nose you have."

Lauren snickered at the comment. She'd thought the same, but she wasn't going to say it aloud. Instead, she added, "Now what?"

John said, "Well, imagine you're a small group of Portuguese soldiers sent here with the king's gold. What would you do with it?" John and Sandra both looked at Lauren like they were instructors testing a new pupil.

Lauren glanced around the pool and speculated. "Well, I wouldn't put it in the water. That would rot a wooden chest or rust an iron barrel. Also, the gold might wash down the slope into the lake. I'd want to bury it." She stomped around the odorous pool, kicking the ground to reveal its composition. Then, she looked up at the sky and continued, "And I'd want to protect it from rain runoff. So, maybe under a rock or overhang."

Surprised by her insight, John said, "That's really very good. Are you sure you haven't done this before?"

"Is it?" Lauren just shrugged, not prepared to reveal more about her expertise than necessary.

Sandra had been exploring on her own while Lauren and John had been talking. She noticed a peculiar spot, brilliantly lit by the sun. She called to the others, "Like this spot over here."

John and Lauren trudged through the vegetation. Sandra pointed at a spot where lava rock formed a small cliff. At the base, the surface turned to soil and was completely grown over with green plants and flowers.

"Ha!" John said in triumph. "Just like that. Good job, honey."

Lauren asked, "So, what do we do now?"

"We dig," John said. He shucked off his backpack and produced a small shovel from inside. "Don't worry, we'll fill the hole back when we're finished. With all the rain here, the plants will be back in a month. No harm done."

"Okay, then." Lauren reached into her own backpack and produced a trowel. Not as effective as the shovel, but she wanted to contribute to the effort.

Soon, they'd created a shallow trench across the face of the rock. John said, "Now, let's see if we can get under the lava's surface. You'd want to tuck the chest under the rock to best protect it."

All three began burrowing sideways into the cliff face. There was loose dirt, which encouraged everyone. After a few minutes, Sandra's shovel hit something hard. "I think I've reached the end of the dirt. It's lava rock again." She thrust her shovel into the hole with force, and all three heard the clinking sound of metal hitting metal.

Looking at Sandra's surprised face, Lauren and John both nodded in excitement. "I think you've found it, dear!" John exclaimed.

All three set to work with renewed energy. Soon, they'd cleared the dirt from the edges of a square object in the hole.

Looking at his wife, John urged her forward and said, "You do the honors."

Sandra leaned into the small hole with both hands. She began rocking the object left and right to dislodge it. Reaching for Lauren's trowel, she pressed the tip behind the object and pried it forward. It was suddenly loosened from its grave, and Sandra fell backward into the foliage, clutching a flat, rectangular object.

Righting herself, she held up a soil-encrusted rock. It was twelve inches wide, four inches high, and flat.

"Did we just pry the face off a chest that's still in there?" Lauren asked, and in the middle of her sentence, her voice seemed to crackle with disbelief.

Brushing the dirt off of the object, Sandra said, "It's got an iron band around it, and it's too heavy to be wood. I'm going to wash it off." She carried the object over to the spring and immersed it under the sulfurous water, brushing it clean with her fingers.

Everyone watched as the moving water carried away layers of dirt and plant roots. What emerged when Sandra pulled it out of the water was a sandstone rock that had clearly been encircled with an iron band. They all ran their fingers over it eagerly.

"What is this?" Sandra asked.

"It's a marker stone," John said. "Stone and iron will last for centuries. They're used to mark the edges of property or the location of something important."

Without waiting for him to finish, Lauren rushed back to the hole and began digging furiously with her trowel.

John and Sandra, ignoring their young and anxious partner, ran their fingers over the surface of the stone and the iron in a mesmerized fashion.

Pointing to the face of the iron, Sandra asked, "What does that look like to you?"

John nodded. "I think it's the *figa* symbol." He raised his eyebrows at his wife, but he was too lost in his own thoughts to articulate them. *Have we really found a treasure? Or is it something less important?*

Motioning to the rock itself, Sandra said, "See these carvings in the stone? Those look like the Azores Islands to me. We're here on São Miguel." She pointed to the right side of the rock. "And there's a little chipped trail to this island on the left. I think that's Faial."

"Yes, I think you're right." The pair stared at each other. "Did we really find something important?"

At that moment, Lauren broke the spell, returning to their spot in front of the pool of water. Returning to the edge of the spring, she announced, "There's nothing else in the hole. No treasure. No chest. Nothing. Just that rock." There had not been a chest like they had predicted, after all, but Lauren's fingers inside her pocket caressed the single golden coin that had been laying inside the hole.

John held the rock up. "You mean—just that map."

Lauren's mouth dropped open as she also recognized the etchings as drawings of the islands.

CHAPTER 8

CELEBRATING

"Here's to a successful treasure hunt!" John raised a glass of champagne, his eyes gleaming with excitement.

Sandra replied, "Here, here! An unusual outcome compared to most of our hunts." Her smile was wide, mirroring the warmth of the hot spring surrounding them.

Lauren raised her glass as well. "And to the next step, where we find more than just a rock." Her voice was filled with hope and determination.

The trio reclined in the beautiful Poça da Dona Beija hot spring, its curated layout a soothing contrast to the rugged spring they'd discovered on the mountainside. The warm waters eased their muscles, and the lush greenery around them provided a serene backdrop.

"I've got pictures of the rock and iron band from every side. We can use it to guide our search when we get to Faial," Sandra said, her voice confident and assured.

"I wish we'd just kept it," Lauren complained, and there was more than a hint of regret in her tone.

Sandra explained, "We've wrestled with that question ourselves, but taking every historical artifact that you stumble on isn't treasure hunting. It's more like cultural pillaging. You end up with a piece of Portuguese history in a glass case in your living room. It looks great at parties, but you feel guilty and dirty inside." Her expression was serious, reflecting the weight of their past actions.

"It sounds like you have some glass cases at home." Lauren raised an eyebrow, curious about their history.

Looking furtively at John, Sandra answered, "We used to, but they weighed on our consciences. Eventually, we shipped them to museums back in the country where we found them. Now, we just have replicas around the house. We'll make a replica of that rock when we get back home."

"But why did you bury it back in the original spot instead of giving it to the government here on São Miguel?" Eager to understand their true motives, Lauren kept prodding instead of changing the topic.

John chuckled. "Well, in this case, it might actually lead to a chest of gold coins. We wouldn't want the government finding that before we did. It would ruin the adventure." His tone was light, but there was an unmistakable glint of excitement in his eyes.

Sandra added, "And the payoff. Gold coins differ from artifacts. Those we can claim. Portugal will take a portion of it, true, but we can keep the majority. Seeing as how it's impossible to sneak several hundred pounds of gold coins through customs, if we ever get that far, we'll follow the official process of claiming lost treasure when we need to." Her voice was practical, reflecting the logistics of such a big discovery.

Lauren's face took on a sheepish look. "Am I part of that 'we?'" she asked. From her expression, she fully expected to be rejected.

"Oh, absolutely. You're our partner now. How does twenty-five percent sound? John and I were the ones who uncovered several clues to get us this far, but you were definitely a big help." Sandra's tone was reassuring, as was the smile she sent Lauren's way.

"Hmm, twenty-five percent of a hundred pounds of gold sounds fantastic. It would pay for my trip and then some." Her mind racing with the possibilities, Lauren grinned back.

John said, "Oh, yes. It would pay for this trip and ten more just like it."

Before she could get too carried away, though, Lauren's logical side remembered a potential problem. "So, what do we say when we link up with the Global Runners group? Do we tell them what we're doing?"

John and Sandra both looked at each other. Finally, Sandra answered, "We've been lucky so far, but the chances of us really finding a treasure are still tiny. We don't even know if the gold is really out here on the islands. But, on the slight chance that it is, I don't think we want to split it among fifty people. Especially since they're vacationers, not treasure hunters like us."

Lauren raised her glass. "Here, here. I vote for that plan."

Three glasses clinked in agreement, signaling an implicit contract between them. They lapsed into silence as the champagne and hot spring washed away the fatigue of the day. Each person disappeared into their own imaginations, picturing what it would be like to become the discoverer, owner, and spender of an entire chest of gold coins.

As John and Sandra relaxed shoulder to shoulder, the warmth of the water amplifying their contentment, Lauren's eyes studied the couple across from her, assessing the situation. She guessed they were twenty years older than her. She realized then that the couple might have been treasure hunting since before she graduated

high school. Stumbling into this pair of experienced adventurers may have been the best thing that had ever happened to her. But would they keep their promise to share the treasure? She didn't want a repeat of what had happened in Israel.

CHAPTER 9

FINALLY REACHING FAIAL

The propellers of the small aircraft whirred to a stop as John, Sandra, and Lauren disembarked onto Faial Island's tarmac. The trio's spirits soared higher than their recent flight, buoyed by the discovery of their first clue. A warm, gentle breeze caressed their faces, carrying with it the faint scent of salt and exotic flowers.

John inhaled deeply, savoring the island air. "Remember," he said, his eyes twinkling with both excitement and caution, "we're all here to relax on vacation. We'll explore the islands with everyone, indulge in sightseeing, savor the local wine, and bask in this slice of paradise." His tone, though trying to sound carefree, carried an undercurrent of tension, a reminder of their secret mission.

Lauren's hazel eyes sparkled with barely contained excitement. She bounced on the balls of her feet, her voice tinged with impatience. "But what about the treasure? When do we search for that? We can't squander this opportunity!" Her fingers unconsciously traced the outline of the clue hidden in her pocket.

Sandra, ever the voice of reason, placed a calming hand on Lauren's shoulder. Her serene demeanor was a stark contrast to Lauren's restlessness. "And what exactly would you do? Where would you look? We don't have a solid lead yet." She paused, her gaze drifting to the lush, green hills in the distance. "Just wait. The island will unveil its secrets to us, just as it did to Sebastian's men five centuries ago. Trust me, if this treasure wants to be found, it will show us a clue. If it wishes to remain hidden, no amount of frantic searching will find it." Her words carried the weight of deep conviction, which Lauren found she couldn't argue against.

As they entered the compact airport terminal, a cacophony of voices caught their attention. Sandra's eyes lit up with recognition. "Hey, I think those people are part of our group. I spotted them on the WhatChat this week." She gestured towards a cluster of half a dozen individuals gathered around the baggage carousel. Their high-tech running gear — moisture-wicking fabrics emblazoned with popular brands — was a dead giveaway of their shared passion.

Spotting a very familiar face, Sandra's voice carried across the hall, filled with warm camaraderie. "Oh, I haven't seen you since Japan!"

A chorus of excited shouts echoed through the terminal as faces lit up with recognition. Sandra wasn't the only person rekindling old friendships, it seemed. The disparate travelers gradually coalesced into a lively group, their suitcases creating a symphony of wheels against the pitted floor as they flowed towards the exit.

Suddenly, a gruff voice spoke in Lauren's ear. "Where are you all from?"

Lauren was startled at the unexpected query. She instinctively stepped back, finding herself face-to-face with a weathered man sporting a straw cowboy hat. He leaned lightly on a gnarled wooden cane, and his piercing gaze was fixed on Lauren.

"Umm, everywhere, I think," Lauren replied hesitantly, certain this man wasn't part of their running group.

The stranger's eyes narrowed with curiosity. "You're on an expedition of some sort? For television? Are you naturalists?"

Lauren's guard went up at his incessant questioning. "No. Just tourists. Well, running tourists."

The man's weathered face cracked into a smile that didn't quite reach his eyes. "Where are you staying? Perhaps you need a ride."

Alarm bells rang in Lauren's head. She retreated, her voice clipped when she answered, "No, we don't need a ride. I've got to go." Without waiting for a response, she hurried to catch up with her group, the hairs on the back of her neck still standing on end.

As she approached the tour bus, John's concerned gaze met hers. "Who's your new friend over there?"

Lauren shuddered slightly. "I have no idea. He materialized out of nowhere, asking where I was staying and if I needed a ride."

"Did he offer you candy, too?"

"It wasn't funny, John. It was creepy." Lauren's eyes darted back, searching for the mysterious man, but he had already vanished into the crowd.

John's playful grin softened into a reassuring smile. "Well, stay close to us. We'll shield you from your stalker."

Lauren settled into her seat, which was a few rows in front of the Crismans, her unease gradually dissipating in the warmth of safe company. As the bus pulled away from the curb, a flash of green caught her eye. Across the road, a beat-up pickup truck idled, and perched behind the wheel was a familiar straw cowboy hat. Lauren's breath caught in her throat, but before she could point it out, the bus moved on.

At the front of the bus, Susana, their hostess and tour guide, addressed the group, her melodious voice carrying a hint of an exotic accent. "We'll be dropping you off at the hotel shortly. You can leave your luggage in storage, and then, the afternoon is yours to enjoy. Lounge by the pool, explore our beaches, or wander through the charming town. I highly recommend Peter Café Sport, it's quite famous. Both tourists and locals favor it. Pete also runs an adventure center and a fascinating history museum where you can delve deeper into the rich past of our beautiful island."

John's eyes lit up at the mention of the museum. He turned to Sandra, barely containing his excitement. "Did you catch that? A history museum. That's definitely a place we need to investigate."

Sandra's lips curved into an amused smile as she rolled her eyes affectionately. "Really? You think they'll have an exhibit proclaiming 'Secret stash of gold coins hidden on the island—finders keepers?'"

John's enthusiasm deflated slightly at her teasing. "Well, do you have a better suggestion?" he asked.

"Gold coins? Here on the island?" A hand suddenly appeared from the row behind them, startling them both.

"My apologies. I couldn't help but overhear. I'm Andrew, by the way."

John twisted in his seat, extending his hand as well. "John Crisman, and this is my wife, Sandra."

"Pleasure to meet you both. This is my sister, Amber." The woman in question waved at the Crismans and gave them a shy smile.

Andrew leaned forward, and his voice lowered conspiratorially. "Now, about those gold coins…?"

Sandra shot John a warning look, giving him a meaningful nudge.

Trying to sound nonchalant, John backpedaled. "Oh, you know, the History Channel ran a segment about pirates using these islands as hideouts. They hinted at the possibility of buried treasure. We figured the museum might touch on those legends, too."

"Oh." Andrew's voice dripped with disappointment. "Is that all? I thought it might be something more… substantial."

John attempted to salvage the friendliness of the conversation while also dousing the other man's suspicions. "Well, aren't all documentaries true?"

Andrew's frustration was palpable. "Those shows are all hype and no substance. They build up the excitement but never deliver genuine discoveries. I want to see some genuine treasure, you know?"

John raised an eyebrow, taken aback by the stranger's intense reaction to a casual mention of gold.

Their exchange was cut short as the bus pulled up to an opulent resort. The vehicle erupted into a flurry of activity as everyone scrambled to disembark.

The young siblings flashed friendly smiles. Before leaving, Amber spoke up, her voice warm and inviting, "We'll be seeing you around. Maybe we could visit that museum together later?"

Sandra replied with a polite smile. "Yes, perhaps we could."

As they gathered their belongings, John turned his back to the conversation, his face clouding with concern. The casual invitation from these strangers felt oddly intrusive, given the couple's secret plan on Faial. He exchanged a meaningful glance with Sandra, silently agreeing that they needed to tread carefully. The treasure hunt had barely begun, and already their secret was slipping out.

CHAPTER 10

FIRST RUN

John crested the hill, his lungs burning and legs trembling with exertion. What had begun as a leisurely jog along the picturesque Horta harbor with the Global Runners Travel group had quickly morphed into a grueling, uphill battle against gravity and his own endurance. Sandra had settled into a gentle rhythm at the back of the pack. But John wanted to establish his credentials as a serious runner in the group.

He found himself on the weathered, stone patio of a centuries-old Catholic church, its walls crafted from chunks of volcanic rock that seemed to grow organically from the hillside. The edifice stood as a silent sentinel, its weathered cross proclaiming faith to the entire southern face of the island.

From this elevation, John's gaze swept across a panorama that took his breath away more thoroughly than the climb had. To the south, the vast Atlantic stretched to the horizon, its deep blue waters broken only by the looming silhouette of Pico's massive volcano just across the channel. Directly below, a crescent of golden sand curved gracefully along the coastline, dotted with the colorful specks of early morning beachgoers, their umbrellas looking like exotic flowers blooming on the shore.

Alone at the peak, John's voice was barely above a whisper as he addressed the ghost of history. "King Sebastian, where would your soldiers have hidden the treasure? Is it perched on a mountaintop? Nestled in a protected cove? Or buried beneath the undulating grasslands?"

A voice, punctuated by ragged breaths, startled him from behind. "I don't think"—there was a pause as the speaker gulped for air—"they would have put it in the fields. Too hard to find again."

John turned to see Lauren, her face flushed with exertion, her running clothes clinging to her lithe frame as she joined him on the church patio.

Nodding in agreement, John replied, "You're right. It must be near a natural landmark."

Lauren's brow furrowed as she considered the implications. "A landmark that was obvious 500 years ago could be completely gone today."

John's expression darkened at the thought. "In which case, our treasure hunt is hopeless. We have to assume there's some way to find it besides sheer luck."

With a mischievous glint in her eye, Lauren closed her eyes and raised her arms, swaying left and right as if moved by an unseen force. "Your wife seems to think the magical universe will show it to us. Maybe we should let her reach out for it."

John couldn't help but chuckle. "Not magic. Maybe something like intuition. She's found things before. It makes us a good team."

Realizing she might have overstepped, Lauren backpedaled. "Sorry, I was just kidding around." Her gaze swept across the rugged landscape. "There are several high points. This island was formed by multiple volcanoes over the centuries."

John pointed across the water at the imposing cone of Pico's volcano. "There's no mistaking that one over there, though the map pointed to Faial, not Pico. So, we have to work from here."

Deciding they had gleaned all they could from this vantage point, Lauren's competitive spirit flared. "You ready to finish this run, old man?" Without waiting for an answer, she darted past John and disappeared down the trail, her footfalls echoing off the volcanic rocks.

"Damn!" John muttered as he set off in pursuit.

The pair raced down the hill, the descent a treacherous dance of gravity and control. As they reached level ground, they erupted into an all-out sprint for the last stretch. Lauren reveled in her clear lead, a certain victory within her grasp.

As she rounded the turn onto the beach, her elation morphed into shock. There, parked at the corner, sat a battered, green pickup. The weathered face beneath a straw cowboy hat regarded her from the driver's seat. Meanwhile, a shadowed figure occupied the passenger side. Both pairs of eyes tracked her as she flew past the truck and onto the sand.

She crossed the finish line in an almost panicked dash, leaving John far behind. Gasping for air, she collapsed to her knees as Sheryl, the race director, and several staff members erupted in cheers.

"Great job!" Sheryl exclaimed, but her smile faded into an expression of concern as she noted Lauren's distress. "Are you okay? Do you need water?"

As if conjured by magic, a full cup materialized in Lauren's trembling hand. She gulped it down greedily, still on her knees.

John crossed the finish line moments later, and he was greeted by his own round of congratulations. He immediately made his way to Lauren's side. "You smoked it. You had me even without that last burst of speed."

Lauren looked up at him, her eyes wide with fear. "Did you see it? The green pickup and the creepy guy from the airport? He was waiting down there at the beach turn, just watching us."

John turned to scan the area. "No, I didn't see anything. All I saw was you bolting away from me." He continued to search the beach. "There's nothing there now. Just people enjoying the sun and surf."

Lauren struggled to her feet, though her legs still felt shaky. "He was there. He was watching."

"Why? Is he really a stalker?"

Lauren fixed John with an exasperated look. "No! He knows what we're up to. He wants the treasure if we find it."

John shook his head, and skepticism was evident in his voice when he replied, "How could anyone know? I think you may be a little on edge."

Without another word, Lauren stalked off towards the water, intent on washing away both the sweat of their run and the chill of her growing paranoia with a refreshing swim. As she waded into the cool Atlantic, she couldn't shake the feeling that somewhere, hidden among the beachgoers and tourists, a pair of watchful eyes were still following her every move.

64

DANCE WITH THE BOAT

Pedro, the guide for all things nautical, stood before the gathered runners, a thick book cradled in his weathered hands. His eyes, bright with excitement, swept across the eager faces before him. "Before we board these traditional whaling boats," he began, his voice carrying the lilt of the Azorean accent, "I want to read you a paragraph from an old novel. It is very famous here in the Azores and in America both. Everyone knows Herman Melville's *Moby Dick*?" He paused, watching heads nod in affirmation. "Well, he wrote about American whaling ships at the same time they were visiting the Azores. Here is just one passage from his novel."

Pedro cleared his throat and read, his voice taking on a reverent tone.

> "'Not a few of these whale hunters come from the Azores, where ships from Nantucket, heading to distant seas, frequently dock, to increase the crew with the brave peasants of these rocky islands. It's not quite clear why, but the truth is that the islanders are the best whale hunters.'"

Looking up, Pedro's face beamed with pride. "We are the best whale hunters. So, you can trust the crew of your boat, no doubt about that. Relax and let them teach you to dance with the boat."

Encouraged by Pedro's words, the runners boarded the long, narrow craft. The wooden hull creaked and swayed beneath their feet as they carefully made their way over the sails, oars, and seats to their assigned positions.

Sandra found herself seated next to Lauren, who asked, "You're from Florida. Do you sail?"

"No. Our boat has a motor. This one is like a giant canoe."

Their discussion was interrupted by the boat captain, a stocky man with a shaved head and skin tanned by years

under the Azorean sun. "Pedro explained we are expert whalers. Today, that means whale watching, not whale hunting. The people of the Azores didn't have a history of whale hunting until we picked it up from the Boston whalers who reached this far in the Atlantic to search for the animals."

As he spoke, the captain's hands moved deftly over the rigging, checking and adjusting with practiced ease. "After sailing over 2,000 miles, the sailors would come into these ports seeking supplies and rest. It was the middle of the 1800s, and the young boys here had heard of America. They signed up as crew on the Boston ships and went to sea. They learned the techniques for whaling from the Americans. They also learned how to process a whale and where to sell the products."

He paused the story to give instructions. "We're raising the sail now. The pick is the short beam across the top of the sail. Watch it as it goes up. Don't let it hit you in the head." The crew members worked in perfect synchronization, their movements fluid and precise as the sail rose up the mast, unfurling like a giant wing eager to catch the wind.

As the sail billowed out, filling with a powerful gust, the boat lurched forward. The captain's voice rose above the sudden commotion. "Lean to starboard! Dance with the boat. Feel the movement and flow into balance with it."

The passengers scrambled to comply, their bodies shifting in unison to counterbalance the wind's force. Sandra found herself pressed against Lauren, both women gripping the gunwale as they leaned out over the water.

As the boat found its equilibrium, cutting smoothly through the waves, the captain continued his history lesson. "Some of the Azorean men stayed on the American ships and made homes in Massachusetts. But a few returned, and they taught those here on the islands to hunt and process the whales. Since we were hunting just off these shores, rather than 2,000 miles from home, we didn't need the big ships. We created small boats like this one because they were more economical. Also, our whalers were actually farmers first. They would chase whales as a second source of income. These boats are easy to operate and familiar, even to a farmer."

As the boat glided through the water, Sandra felt a thrill of excitement. The wind whipped through her hair, carrying the salty tang of the sea. She marveled at how the small craft responded to the slightest adjustment of the sail or shift in weight distribution. It was, indeed, a dance, a delicate balance between human skill and the raw power of nature.

Lauren leaned in close, and even so, her voice was barely audible above the wind and waves. "You know, this boat ride reminds me of treasure hunting."

Sandra's eyebrows shot up in surprise. "How so?"

Lauren grinned, her eyes sparkling with enthusiasm. "Think about it. Those old whalers, they were like treasure hunters of the sea. They'd sail for hours, days, or months, searching for their prize: the whales. When they finally found one, they had to work together, using all their skills and knowledge to catch it. It's not so different from what we're doing here, is it? Searching for hidden treasures, using our skills to guide us."

Sandra nodded slowly as a new perspective dawned on her. "I never thought of it that way, but you're right. And like whaling, if you're successful, you can get rich."

"Exactly," Lauren agreed. "Plus, just like we're learning to 'dance with the boat' today, we need to learn to dance with the clues in our treasure hunt. Sometimes, we need to adjust our course, and sometimes, we need to work together to balance things out. But we always need to stay in tune with our environment and our instincts."

As the boat sailed on, Sandra saw their adventure in a new light. The rhythmic creaking of the boat, the snap of the sail in the wind, and the steady splash of waves against the hull seemed to whisper secrets of forgotten histories. She realized that this sailing experience wasn't just a tourist activity—it was a lesson in the very skills they would need to uncover the treasures they sought.

CHAPTER 12

SHOPPING SURPRISE

The morning sun glinted off the azure waters of Horta's harbor as Sandra, Lauren, and John stepped out of their quaint hotel. The air was crisp and salty, carrying the sound of gently lapping waves against the marina's edge.

Sandra turned to John, her blonde hair whipping in the sea breeze. "John, Lauren and I are going shopping. We're browsing all the shops along the waterfront." When John stepped forward as if to join them, she added, her voice softening, "You can stay here at the hotel or go looking for treasure clues."

John's shoulders slumped, his usually energetic demeanor dampened by the exclusion. He mumbled an acknowledgment and trudged back into the hotel, his footsteps echoing on the worn cobblestones.

Once out of earshot, Sandra confided to Lauren, her voice barely above a whisper, "I need some relaxation. We don't have to work all the time on vacation. Let's see what we can find."

Lauren nodded, her dark eyes scanning the colorful storefronts lining the street. She hadn't expected a genuine friendship to emerge from her partnership with the Crismans. She still saw them as both allies and competitors in their quest.

As they meandered through the narrow streets, the scent of freshly baked queijadas wafted from a nearby café. They dipped into the charming boutiques that dotted the waterfront, each a treasure trove of local craftsmanship.

In one shop, its walls adorned with intricate tapestries depicting whaling scenes, Sandra exclaimed, "Look at these beautiful earrings!" She held up a pair of delicate, white, petal-shaped ornaments. "They look like stone or mother-of-pearl, but they're actually made from the inner meat of a fig branch."

Lauren's eyebrows shot up in surprise. "How is that possible?" she wondered aloud, carefully examining the earrings. "This artist must be a genius. Here's a little card explaining the process."

Sandra beamed, and her eyes twinkled with excitement. "Nothing like that in the States, is there?"

Lauren held up another piece, this one a necklace that shimmered in the soft light of the shop. "How about this necklace made from fish scales? You'd swear it was coral."

After purchasing both pieces of jewelry, scented soap infused with local lavender, and a piece of exquisite Azorean embroidery, the two women continued their stroll. The cobblestone streets led them past whitewashed buildings with terracotta roofs, their facades occasionally interrupted by vibrant splashes of bougainvillea.

As they rounded a corner, Lauren's eyes sparkled in recognition. She pointed to a weathered building with a faded painted sign. "Hey, that's Peter Café Sport! It's been here for over a hundred years. We have to stop in for their famous gin and tonic."

Sandra nodded eagerly. "I'm game. I could use a break from shopping."

They entered the café and were immediately enveloped by the warm buzz of conversation and the rich aroma of coffee. The walls were adorned with maritime memorabilia like old photographs, ship models, and colorful flags from vessels that had docked in Horta over the decades.

As they sipped their perfectly crafted gin and tonics, Sandra's gaze wandered around the room, taking in the eclectic decor. Her eyes fell on a worn, wooden door at the back, its faded letters spelling out "Scrimshaw Museum." Turning to Lauren, she said, "Now, that's something original we have to look into."

Lauren followed Sandra's gaze and asked, "What's scrimshaw?"

Sandra paused in surprise, then educated her young companion. "For centuries, sailors were away at sea for months at a time. They needed a hobby to keep them busy, like giving each other tattoos. Well, scrimshaw is like a tattoo but on the teeth or bones of whales. A sailor would take an entire tooth or just fragments of one, then carve a scene into it with a knife. Initially, they might have been pretty crude. But with months and years of practice, some sailors became excellent artists. They would do portraits of their shipmates, girlfriends, whaling scenes, mermaids—anything, really."

"Like ivory carving in Africa," Lauren mused.

"Yes, similar, but also completely different. Let's go have a look."

Finishing their drinks, they ascended the creaky wooden stairs at the back of the café. On the second floor, they found themselves in a scene that amazed them both. The museum wasn't a small collection on dusty shelves, but a treasure trove of artistry. Hundreds of pieces were professionally mounted and displayed in gleaming glass

cases, the soft lighting bringing out the intricate details of each carving.

Sandra's voice was hushed with awe. "I've never seen anything like this. Other museums might have one or two pieces to show the art form, but there are hundreds here."

Lauren nodded, but then, her attention was captured by a particularly striking piece. She pointed at a tooth engraved with a detailed picture of a battle between a sperm whale and a giant squid. "And they're beautiful," she added. "How can anyone be that precise with a knife and their bare hands? This seems impossible."

"Time to practice, over and over again until you're a master," Sandra replied, her fingers hovering just above the glass case.

They moved from one piece to another, each calling for the attention of the other when they found one that was particularly dramatic. There were portraits of weathered sailors, longing lovers, solemn religious figures, and famous people from history. The theme was usually nautical, with scenes depicting sailing ships, ship's equipment, and the majestic whales themselves.

As they explored, Lauren's gaze fell on a less ornate piece. "Sandra, look at this one," she called out. "It's different from the others."

Sandra leaned down to inspect the carving. The surface of the tooth was mostly untouched, containing just nine small blotches. "It's a map of the Azores Islands," she realized. "Corvo is far off to the west. São Miguel and Santa Maria are to the east. And here we are on Faial."

Lauren added, "And look at that volcano across the water."

"That's Pico, the highest volcano in the archipelago. We've been looking at it every day since we've been here."

"Mm-hm. I know that. But what's up on the peak of the volcano?"

Sandra squinted. "Just a jagged edge?"

"That's not what the peak looks like in real life. I think that jagged top looks like a crown. Doesn't it?"

As understanding dawned, Sandra's eyes widened. "It sure does. Why would that be there? Pico Island was never the capital or even the major trading hub of the Azores."

"Something royal?" Lauren offered.

Sandra's mind raced with possibilities. "No. It couldn't be."

Lauren challenged, "Why not?"

"Well, primarily because these were all carved in the 1800s or 1900s. Sebastian's treasure was hidden in the 1500s."

Lauren wasn't ready to give up hope just yet. "Maybe this sailor was copying an older map that he'd seen."

Her curiosity officially piqued, Sandra conceded that Lauren had a fair point. "Let's see if we can get any more details on this piece."

As they sought the museum curator, both women felt a surge of anticipation. Lauren found her fingers dancing along the outer edges of her thighs, and her mind raced with the possibilities. *Can this unassuming scrimshaw piece be the key to unlocking the next stage of our treasure hunt?* The creaking floorboards beneath their feet and the silent witnesses of centuries-old whale teeth seemed to whisper secrets of hidden treasures and forgotten histories. Their shopping trip was about to take an unexpected turn. She could just feel it.

Sandra approached the curator, who was a tall, elegant woman with deep mahogany skin and silver-streaked hair pulled back in a neat bun. Her crisp, white blouse and dark skirt exuded professionalism, while a delicate scarf adorned with nautical motifs hinted at her passion for maritime history.

"Excuse me, ma'am," Sandra began, "can you tell us anything about the origins of this piece?"

The curator's eyes lit up as she glided over to join them, her slight British accent a melodic surprise. "Ah, you've found one of our most intriguing pieces. We affectionately call it 'King Pico.' I see you've noticed the crown atop the mountain?"

Sandra nodded eagerly. "Yes, that's exactly what caught our attention. Why would there be a crown on top of the volcano?"

The curator's lips curved into a knowing smile. She leaned in slightly, as if about to share a secret. "Well, the first and most widely believed explanation is that Pico, being the largest volcano in the archipelago, is the king of them all." She paused, her eyes twinkling, before continuing in a playful tone, "It's a simple and logical explanation—but it is wrong."

Lauren's eyebrows shot up at the assertion. "Oh? You sound very certain about that."

"Indeed I am," the curator replied, her voice becoming more serious. "That is a very special crown on the volcano. Notice its unique shape. It's not your typical royal headpiece. Instead, it's a nine-pointed crown, a design created in the 1500s by the treasury of King Sebastian himself. It was used to mark coins and gold bars reserved for the royal treasury, never to be spent."

Sandra, her investigative instincts kicking in, interjected, "But the crown is from the 1500s, and according to the sign here," she said as she gestured towards a small printed description inside the glass, "this scrimshaw wasn't carved until 1856. That's a gap of three centuries. Why would a sailor use such an old symbol?"

The curator's expression tightened slightly at the interruption, but she maintained her composure. "An excellent observation," she acknowledged. "This piece was a prized possession of Naval Captain Pedro Costa.

His family had a long, illustrious history of serving in the royal navy, with ancestors who were ship captains under King Sebastian himself. Captain Costa claimed to have copied this design from maps passed down through generations of his family."

Lauren asked the obvious question. "If it was so precious to him, why would Captain Costa give it to the museum?"

A shadow of sadness passed over the curator's face. "Ah, but he didn't, my dear. Captain Costa met a tragic end at sea. His family, left in dire straits, sold what they could to finance their emigration to America. Our founder acquired this piece, along with several others, for our collection."

Sandra and Lauren exchanged a meaningful glance. "Others from the same family?" Sandra probed. "Are they on display here as well?"

The curator nodded, gesturing towards the case before them. "Indeed, they are. Most of the pieces you see here are from Captain Costa's collection."

"You've been incredibly helpful," Sandra said warmly before raising her phone. "Would it be alright if I took a few pictures of the map on the whale's tooth?"

"Of course," the curator replied. "We encourage visitors to capture memories of their visit."

As the curator drifted away to assist other patrons, Sandra turned to Lauren, her voice low and urgent. "I think you might be onto something. This could very well be pointing to Sebastian's treasure."

Lauren, already examining the other pieces in the case, suddenly gestured to a scrimshaw depicting a forested scene before a rocky cliff. "Sandra, look at this one. There's something unusual here."

Sandra leaned in with a furrowed brow. "Unusual? Where? I just see trees and the cliff."

"It's subtle," Lauren explained, her finger hovering over a specific point. "But isn't that a crown inscribed on the cliff face?"

Sandra quickly snapped a picture and zoomed in on her phone screen, panning left and right. Lauren's finger traced over a spot on the display. "There!"

Sandra's eyes widened as she saw it, too. "It certainly looks like it. So, does this mean that somewhere on the volcano, there's a cliff in the forest where the treasure is hidden?"

Lauren's eyes sparkled with excitement, like when she discovered the single gold coin on São Miguel. "Yes, it has to be. What else could it mean?"

Sandra took several more pictures, carefully capturing each piece in the Costa collection. She lowered her voice to a whisper when she said, "There might be more clues here that we're overlooking. We should show these to John and get his opinion."

As they slipped out of the museum, Lauren, caught up in the moment, bid farewell to the proprietor in Portuguese, *"Bom dia, minha senhora."*

The pair hurried down the creaky stairs, their minds abuzz with the possibilities that lay before them. The salty sea air hit them as they exited Peter Café Sport, carrying with it the suggestion of adventure on the slopes of Pico volcano.

CHAPTER 13

DARK FIGURES

The sun had dipped below the horizon, painting the sky in deep purples and oranges as twilight settled over Faial Island. John Crisman had been just as excited by the discovery at the scrimshaw museum. After they brought him up to speed on their plan, Lauren sat outside at the resort, trying to relax as the day faded into night. The gentle lapping of waves against the distant docks provided a soothing backdrop.

As darkness crept across the landscape, the shadows seemed to deepen, concealing unseen dangers. The scent of exotic flowers filled the air, a stark contrast to the menace that was about to unfold. Lauren's momentary peace was shattered by a gravelly voice emerging from the gloom.

"*Bom dia, Senhora* Banister."

A figure emerged from the shadows. Lauren's heart leapt into her throat, and adrenaline surged through her veins. The dark, leathery face stared at her impassively from beneath the ever-present cowboy hat, and the man's eyes were cold and calculating.

"Whaaa!" Lauren startled and leapt to her feet, her body tensing for fight or flight. "Who are you? Why are you following me?"

The leathery face didn't answer her, its silence more unnerving than any response could have been. Instead, a second figure emerged from the shadows, his familiar voice sending a chill down Lauren's spine.

"Hello, Lauren, it's good to see you again."

"Victor!" Lauren gasped as her mind raced to piece together this unexpected puzzle. She glanced sideways at the older man, suddenly feeling trapped between two potential threats. "You're working with him?"

Victor stepped closer, and his charming smile was at odds with the menacing atmosphere. "Honey, this is my colleague, Duarte Escobar. We…" He wasn't able to finish the sentence, however.

Lauren snapped back, her voice sharp with anger and fear, "Don't 'honey' me. We're through. We've been through ever since you cheated me out of my share of the Israel documents."

"Don't be that way. It was an accident. I can make it up to you," Victor tried to defend himself, but his words rang hollow in the tense night air.

Lauren turned to the leather-faced man, and the whole time, her instincts screamed about the danger she faced. "You can't trust him. A partnership means nothing to him. He'll cheat you as soon as he gets a chance."

Duarte Escobar showed no expression, but his response sent ice through Lauren's veins. "He won't cheat me out of anything. Not if he wants to continue breathing."

The ice-cold tone of the voice told her everything about the type of man Victor had partnered with. She was alone, cornered by two men—one a betrayer, the other clearly dangerous—with no immediate help in sight.

"What do you want?" She directed at her former lover.

Victor replied, his casual tone belying the gravity of the situation, "We want the same thing you want."

"A relaxing vacation on a beautiful island?" Her attempt at humor wasn't enough to slow her racing heart.

Victor laughed aloud, and the sound echoed ominously in the otherwise quiet night. "Oh, please. Honey, I don't believe that for a minute. You're looking for

Sebastian's gold, just like we discussed years ago. That's what we're looking for as well."

Lauren looked around, searching for a way out of this dangerous confrontation, but she knew she had to keep the men talking if she had any hope of coming out of the situation unharmed. "I'm on vacation with this big group of runners." She waved her arm to indicate the surrounding bungalows, to suggest that people were watching this exchange.

"Excellent cover story, honey, but we both know you came here with one clue and a bucket full of hope that you could unravel our 500-year-old mystery," Victor said, his words dripping with condescension.

"I'm not your honey. And it's not 'our' mystery. What makes you think anyone could find it after all this time?"

Victor's next words sent a wave of panic through her. "Just maybe that old couple you're traveling with got a real clue from Emilio's shop in Lisbon." Lauren frowned at the mention of the Crismans, and Victor continued, "Yes, I saw them enter the shop. I'd already been there, and that old man wouldn't tell me anything. But then, they came out filled with excitement. He told them something. I just know it."

Escobar, who had been quiet until this moment, spoke with an undercurrent of menace that made Lauren shudder. "*Senhor* Emilio's family is the key to finding the treasure. Yet, he tells nothing to the serious treasure hunters."

Victor picked up the conversation, and his excitement was palpable and frightening. "So, I started keeping tabs on them. And imagine my surprise when they came traipsing out of the forest on São Miguel with you at their side. That's when I knew what you were doing. So, now, we both find ourselves on Faial Island."

The bungalows surrounding them seemed like distant, unreachable sanctuaries. Lauren realized that her adventure had taken a dangerous turn, and the race for Sebastian's gold had become a matter of life and death.

At that moment, a pair of figures appeared in the courtyard and called out, their voices a lifeline in the oppressive night. Amber shouted, "Lauren! We're going to dinner. Care to join us?"

Lauren glared at Victor and Escobar, her eyes conveying a mixture of defiance and fear. Then, she shouted back, relief evident in her voice, "Yes, absolutely! I'm coming!" Before walking away, she said in a low voice to her former lover, "I'm going back to my vacation now. You can find the gold yourself. Oh, and by the way, we'll be running again tomorrow. It's part of the agenda, not some secret plan to search the forests."

With that, she turned to catch up with her new running friends, her heart pounding with each step. The tranquil beauty of Faial Island had suddenly become sinister, its lush landscapes and secluded beaches now potential hiding places for ruthless competitors.

From behind her, she heard Victor's voice whisper a promise laden with foreboding, "See you later, honey."

Another chill ran down her spine. As Lauren hurried away, she knew with certainty that this encounter was far from over. The night air, once warm and inviting, now felt oppressive and threatening, carrying with it the weight of impending danger.

VOLCANO RUN

The morning sun cast a golden glow over Faial Island as the group of Global Runners gathered at the starting line. The air was crisp and tinged with the scent of volcanic soil and distant ocean spray. Anticipation buzzed through the crowd, each runner bouncing on their toes, eager to tackle the challenging course ahead.

"Global Runners…Go!" Sheryl shouted into the microphone.

With those words, the group surged forward like a herd of wild horses, their energy palpable as they began their first ascent. The Capelo Capelinhos, a string of small volcanoes, stretched before them, promising a grueling, yet exhilarating adventure.

Lauren found herself in the middle of the pack, with her mind elsewhere as her feet automatically navigated the increasingly steep terrain. The events of the previous night weighed heavily on her. Memories of Victor flooded back—their shared passion for adventure, their thrill over uncovering lost treasures, and the intensity of their relationship. For two years, it had been perfect. But then came the betrayal, shattering everything they had built together.

The trail narrowed as it wound up the volcano's flank. Loose scree shifted underfoot, demanding constant attention from the runners, yet Lauren's focus remained inward. She grappled with the stark reality that Victor had only grown more ruthless since their parting.

"What's up, kid? You seem distracted." John's voice broke through her reverie as he fell into step beside her. His face showed concern beneath the sheen of sweat from the climb.

Lauren hesitated, unwilling to burden her new friend with the danger that had found her. "Oh, hey. Nothing. I'm just thinking about where to start our search on Pico Island."

His enthusiasm evident, despite the exertion of the climb, John shared his plan. Lauren was just thankful that he didn't continue to question her about her mood. "I thought that once we get over there, we can ask around about Captain Costa and maybe show the picture to some guides."

Their conversation was interrupted as Stacy, another runner from the group, caught up to them. Her short, blonde ponytail bobbed with each determined stride. "What are you two talking about?"

John, ever quick on his feet, deflected. "We're worried about how steep that climb is." He gestured towards the imposing incline ahead.

"Let's move. We'll tackle it together," Stacy encouraged, her competitive spirit infectious.

The next section of the trail proved brutally steep. Conversation ceased as the runners focused all their energy on the grueling ascent. Lauren's mind drifted once more to the past, to the incident with the ancient Jewish scrolls that had ended her relationship with Victor.

As they crested the ridge, the group was rewarded with a breathtaking vista. A verdant valley spread out before them, untouched by human development. Vibrant hibiscus bloomed at their feet in a riot of blue, pink, and white, while purple flowering vines twisted through the trees lining the path.

"Wow! That's beautiful," Lauren exclaimed as she took in the view.

John, his phone raised to capture the moment, commented between deep breaths, "That's one climb behind us. Only two more to go. Look at that forest. You could hide a chest of gold anywhere in there, and no one would ever find it."

Lauren countered, drawing on her expertise to do so. "You certainly could. But without a permanent landmark or modern GPS, you wouldn't be able to find it again. Most places in this terrain are terrible hiding places, unless you really do intend for it to be lost forever."

The group continued their journey, tackling each rise and fall of the landscape. As they emerged from the forest, the scenery changed dramatically. The lush vegetation gave way abruptly to a vast expanse of barren rock formations, the swirls of recent lava flows etched into the brown and gray stone faces.

"Lauren! This is what the lava fields in Iceland look like. It feels like we've been transported to a different continent," John called out, awe clear in his voice.

"It's stunning, but such a striking change," Lauren agreed, and she marveled at the stark beauty of the volcanic landscape before her.

The last climb took them up the most recently active volcano, which had erupted continuously from 1957 to 1958. From its peak, they gazed out over land that had existed for barely half a century, born from the fiery depths of the Earth. This eruption was the event that had finally pushed half the population off Faial Island. They had to immigrate to the United States to escape the suffocating layers of volcanic ash.

The descent was a wild, exhilarating rush down the volcano's sand-covered slope. Lauren's speed proved both an advantage and a liability as she lost control and tumbled into the loose earth. John loped past, claiming victory at the finish line, with Lauren close on his heels.

As they joined the raucous celebration at the end, dancing to blasting music, Lauren felt a moment of pure joy. The thrill of the run, the beauty of the island, and the camaraderie of her fellow runners momentarily eclipsed her worries. Yet, as the adrenaline faded, she couldn't shake the feeling that a menacing shadow was following her.

NEW EARTH

John, Sandra, and Lauren gathered their thoughts after an exhilarating race across three volcanoes. The day's adventure had sparked an idea, a potential key to narrowing their search for Sebastian's elusive treasure.

John approached Susana, their lead tour guide, who was busy checking her phone for messages. Her hair was slightly disheveled from the day's activities, but her eyes still sparkled with energy.

"Susana," John began, his voice filled with genuine enthusiasm, "that was an incredible race. It's really

inspired me to learn more about these volcanoes and their history."

Susana looked up, a pleased smile spreading across her face. "That's wonderful to hear, John. What kind of details are you interested in?"

John exchanged a quick glance with Sandra before continuing. "We've been fascinated by your descriptions of the volcanoes. We'd love to get some more scientific, geological information about how these islands formed. I understand the University of the Azores has a major department studying the volcanoes. Would it be possible to talk to one of their professors?"

Susana's eyes lit up at the suggestion. "Oh, absolutely! In fact, my neighbor's uncle is a geology professor at the university. He lives right here on Faial Island. Would you like to meet him?"

John could barely contain his excitement, but he tried to keep his voice casual. "Yes, I would like that very much. If it's not too much of an imposition, of course."

Susana's brow furrowed in thought for a moment, her lips pursed. Suddenly, her face brightened. "Ah-ha! I have it. Tonight, we'll all dine at the Oceanic. It's a wonderful restaurant. I'm sure you'll love it. The professor is also a fan of the food there. I'll invite him to join us for dinner, and you can talk with him as long as you like." She paused, remembering a slight detail she needed to mention. "But, of course, you'll have to cover his food and drink. We can't pay from Global Runners' account."

John nodded eagerly. "Yes, absolutely! We'd be happy to take care of that. Can you tell me his name?"

Susana was already typing furiously on her phone. "He's Dr. Luis Azevedo. He's a graduate of the Universidade de Lisboa, where he studied geology and geodynamics. He's the best in the country."

John, Sandra, and Lauren exchanged excited glances as Susana continued her rapid-fire texting. After a few moments, she looked up with a triumphant smile. "Excellent! He'll meet us at the Oceanic at seven tonight."

∽ ∽ ∽

The Oceanic restaurant lived up to its reputation. The warm, inviting atmosphere was enhanced by the gentle sound of waves lapping at the nearby docks. The group had settled at a large, round table near a window overlooking the darkening ocean. A spread of local cheeses, olives, and a bottle of glistening white wine adorned the table's center.

Dr. Azevedo, a man in his early forties with salt-and-pepper hair and thick-rimmed glasses, needed little encouragement to expound on his favorite subject. John had specified that he was interested in eruptions since the

1500s, a request that Azevedo had taken as an intriguing challenge rather than questioning its oddity.

As Azevedo launched into his lecture, John couldn't help but notice the professor's animated gestures and the way his eyes lit up behind his glasses. The man was clearly in his element.

"Now, let's begin with Faial," Azevedo said while pouring himself a glass of wine. "There have been only two eruptions here since 1500. The first was in 1672, occurring in the Capelo Volcanic Complex."

He paused, taking a sip of wine before continuing. "This eruption was quite the spectacle, characterized by both explosive and effusive activity. It began with phreato-magmatic explosions—that's when magma interacts with water, creating violent steam explosions. These produced significant amounts of ash and carved out a new crater."

Azevedo's hands moved animatedly as he spoke, mimicking the explosion. "As the eruption progressed, it transitioned to more effusive activity, generating lava flows that extended the island's coastline."

Noticing the slight confusion on Lauren's face, Azevedo backtracked. "Perhaps I should define some terms. 'Effusive' means that the volcano pushed thick, molten lava up to the surface, and it flowed across the land like a river. 'Explosive,' on the other hand, means that the magma was thinner and had more gas, so an

eruption could launch it into the sky. Quite majestic. The Capelo event exhibited both behaviors."

John nodded, absorbing the information while trying to hide his impatience to hear about Pico's volcano.

Azevedo continued, and all the while, his enthusiasm grew. "Then, we have the most recent and arguably most famous volcanic event on Faial Island. The Capelinhos eruption." He leaned forward, his voice lowering dramatically, and he had a grin forming on his face. "This event occurred from September 27th, 1957, to October 24th, 1958."

The professor paused, making eye contact with each of his listeners to ensure they had registered the specific dates. Satisfied that they had, he continued, "This eruption was truly remarkable. It began as a submarine event, with initial explosions occurring just off the western coast. As it continued, it built up an entirely new peninsula, eventually connecting to the existing island."

Sandra's eyes widened in realization. "That's where we were running this morning, isn't it? All that barren, rocky terrain? We watched an old video of the event in the underground museum."

Azevedo beamed at her observation. "Precisely! All of that land you raced on was created by this eruption. It's fascinating, isn't it? To think you were running on earth that didn't exist just sixty-five years ago."

He motioned to the server, who promptly refilled his wineglass. "Interestingly," he continued after taking a sip, "the new land was even more extensive immediately after the eruption. Sadly, over sixty percent of it has been carried away by winds and ocean currents over the decades."

Lauren, who had been listening intently but growing increasingly impatient, saw an opportunity to steer the conversation in another direction. "But what about eruptions of Pico? Did those occur simultaneously with the ones on Faial?"

Azevedo's eyes sparkled at the question. "Ah, an excellent query! One might assume so, given the proximity of the two islands. But nature often surprises us." He leaned back in his chair, swirling the wine in his glass. "In fact, the eruptions on Pico occurred at very different times. The activity in one location typically relieves the underground pressure."

He set down his glass and leaned forward, his voice taking on a more serious tone. "The most significant eruptions of Pico volcano since 1500 occurred between 1562 and 1564. This one took place on the southeast flank of the volcano, in an area known as the Mistério da Prainha."

John's interest piqued noticeably at this information.

"Like the eruption on Faial," Azevedo said, "it was both explosive and effusive activity." He raised an eyebrow, searching his audience's faces to see if they understood.

All three nodded, remembering the terms he'd explained earlier.

"The eruption began with explosive phases, producing ash and scoria—that's volcanic rock full of gas bubbles. It then transitioned to more effusive activity, generating substantial lava flows that reached the coast and expanded the island's land area."

Azevedo's eyes gleamed as he described the landscape. "These lava flows created a rugged, almost lunar landscape that's still visible today. Locals refer to these areas as 'mistérios'—mysteries—because of their otherworldly appearance."

He waited until they all gestured for him to keep going, but he snuck another sip of wine before he did so. "Of course, this eruption had a significant impact on the island's inhabitants. While there were no recorded fatalities, the lava flows destroyed agricultural land and some settlements, forcing local populations to relocate."

John, barely able to contain his curiosity, raised a finger for a question. "Did this lava cover the entire island of Pico?" He tried to keep his voice neutral, but there was an undercurrent of anxiety. Lauren understood what he was feeling, as that same anxiousness was clawing at her stomach.

Azevedo chuckled and shook his head. "Oh, no, certainly not. This eruption affected just the southeastern section of the island. If you visit, you can still find the lines showing the edges of the lava flow. I've explored them myself, you know."

John visibly relaxed, relief clear in his voice when he said, "That's good to hear. I was worried the locals might have been left with nowhere to go."

Azevedo nodded, then straightened in his chair, preparing to continue his lecture. "Now, the second notable eruption occurred in 1718, again on the southeast flank of the volcano. This event was smaller compared to the one that occurred in 1562, but it still produced lava flows that reached the coast. The affected area is known as the Mistério de Santa Luzia."

As Azevedo delved into more technical details about lava composition and his personal explorations of the mountain, John's mind wandered. He had the information he needed to continue their search on Pico Island. Glancing at Sandra and Lauren, he could see they were thinking the same thing. Their next step was clear—they needed to get to Pico.

SHADOWS IN PARADISE

The Maresia Bar, nestled in a narrow cobblestone street of Horta on Faial Island, was a haven for locals and the occasional adventurous tourist. Its weather-beaten facade, painted a faded blue to match the Azorean sky, barely hinted at the intrigue brewing within its dim interior.

Duarte Escobar, a man whose very presence seemed to chill the tropical air, sat in a secluded corner. His dark eyes, hard as volcanic glass, scanned the room ceaselessly, missing nothing. "I want to know exactly what she's planning. Where is she searching? Where will she go next?" Escobar's voice was low, but it carried the unmistakable edge of a man accustomed to the absolute obedience of others.

Across the wooden table, Victor shifted uncomfortably in his seat. Sweat beaded on his forehead, not entirely because of the humid evening air. "You will. Right now, it looks like she's just running and hanging out with the travel group. I don't know if she's trying to throw us off her track, or she just doesn't have any idea where to look."

Victor's mind drifted to Lauren, his former girlfriend. The memory of her hurt expression when he'd left her still haunted him, but the weight of the payout in his pocket had dulled the sting.

The surrounding bar hummed with quiet conversation and the clinking of glasses. Local fishermen shared tales over glasses of Especial beer, while a group of German hikers excitedly planned their trek around the islands. The scent of grilled limpets and fresh bread wafted from the kitchen, mingling with the ever-present salty tang of the ocean.

Escobar lifted his glass of aged rum, the amber liquid catching the light from the wrought-iron chandelier above. "When will your mole be here?"

"Five more minutes," Victor assured him, glancing nervously at his watch. "She'll know more about the situation, I promise."

"She'd better." Escobar's gaze swept across the room once more, assessing each patron as a potential asset or threat, and his scowl looked powerful enough to make the tropical air feel chilly.

The door creaked open, admitting a gust of fresh air and a young woman. Stacy Mason entered, her confident stride belying the apprehension in her eyes as she spotted Victor and his imposing companion.

Eager to make the introduction and get Escobar's focus off of him, Victor leapt to his feet and opened his arms wide. "*Senhor* Escobar, this is Stacy Mason. She's part of the Global Runners tourist group." Turning to Stacy, he continued, "Stacy, this is Duarte Escobar. He's funding this expedition."

Stacy extended her hand, a gesture Escobar pointedly ignored. She lowered it slowly, her smile faltering, and she took in the cold, calculating look in Escobar's eyes.

As Stacy settled into her seat, the gravity of the situation seemed to press down on her. The quaint bar, with its walls adorned with photographs of whaling ships and nautical instruments, suddenly felt claustrophobic.

Escobar broke the tense silence. ""Did he tell you what we need you to do?"

Stacy looked at Victor, then back at Escobar. "Just keep an eye on the group. Let you know where we're going. Who we meet locally."

"Yes, that's basically it. But more specifically, we need to know what Lauren Banister is doing. The others don't matter. Does she explore off on her own? Who does she meet with during the trip? We need to know what she's planning to do before she does it."

Stacy understood. "So, I need to strike up a friendship with Lauren. Stay close to her. Ask questions. Then relay any information I find out back to you. Or Victor."

"Yes, relay back to Victor," Escobar agreed.

"And in exchange, I will receive…what, exactly?" She looked at Victor for the answer. She wasn't comfortable addressing this question to Escobar, in case he took it the wrong way.

Victor gave her a warm smile. "For this tiny amount of help, we will pay you a minimum of ten thousand dollars." Victor let that number sink in. Then, he added, "But if you can be more helpful, there will be a bonus waiting for you."

Stacy's mind began thinking about how she could use that kind of cash. There were so many credit card bills. "That sounds fine to me."

Victor looked to Escobar for his approval. He received no sign in return. Turning to Stacy, he said, "Well, perhaps we could get the first report tomorrow evening?"

Eager to show her efficiency, Stacy countered with, "Or I could give you my first report right now."

Both men exchanged surprised looks, then turned their full attention to the young woman. Victor asked, "You have something now?"

As dinner in the Oceanic restaurant had progressed, Stacy had been drawn to the very energetic and animated conversation at the table next to her. She'd turned her chair to listen to the detailed lecture about volcanic activities on the islands. She had eavesdropped on most of what was said by the geology professor, Lauren Banister, and the Crismans.

When *Senhor* Escobar had named the person who they were interested in, she knew that the professor and the lecture were related to the job they wanted. She recounted everything she'd heard and filled in some pieces she'd missed with her own guesses. Seeking to give as much detail as possible, her first report took almost ten minutes to convey. When she finished, she saw the slightest smile on Escobar's face, the only positive expression he'd shown during the entire meeting.

Victor sat in astonishment at the richness of the story he'd just heard. Finally, he said, "That…that's exactly what we wanted to know. Umm, and of course, anything more along those lines."

Pleased with herself, Stacy smiled at Victor as sweetly as she could manage. "You mentioned a bonus. Perhaps delivering that kind of information before I was even hired justifies a bonus. I could use a couple of hundred now to help with shopping." She waited for Victor to react.

Victor looked at Escobar, who nodded slightly. Victor reached into his pocket and pulled out a folded pad of euros. Counting it out, he said, "I can give you two hundred now."

Assessing the pile of cash, Stacy countered with, "I think three hundred would work better." Victor peeled off some additional bills and handed them to her across the table.

Stacy looked at the men, waiting for further instructions. When neither spoke, she stood and said, "Wonderful doing business with you. I'll have something more for you tomorrow evening." Then she walked out of the bar, much more confidently than she had entered.

When Stacy departed, a subtle shift had occurred. Escobar's gaze lingered on her retreating form before turning back to Victor. "I like her."

As night settled over Faial, the quaint bar returned to its usual rhythm, unaware of the dark undercurrents that had just rippled through its cozy confines.

CHAPTER 17

PERILOUS WATERS

The morning sky hung heavy with clouds as the ferry to Pico Island swayed gently at the Horta dock. The sky was growing gray, and the air was thick with the scent of impending rain, a stark contrast to the excited chatter of tourists boarding the vessel. Among them, John, Sandra, and Lauren huddled close, their voices low as they discussed their recent revelations.

"You realize what we learned last night?" John whispered as his eyes darted around to ensure their privacy.

Sandra nodded, and she replied in a hushed voice, "Umm, that the treasure could be buried under layers of lava?"

"Or that the southwest side of the island is not worth searching," Lauren chimed in.

Sandra looked back at the younger woman. "Clearly. Because it was covered in lava…twice."

Lauren continued, "Yes, that's right, but it's more than that. The scrimshaw images are more recent than the volcanic eruptions. So, that suggests that the markers to the treasure location still existed when they were carved, and that rules out the southwest side. But it also means the treasure wasn't buried."

John nodded. "That seems probable to me. It's not a guarantee, but it gives me hope that it's still accessible somewhere."

As they boarded, the ferry's metal gangway creaked under their feet, the sound nearly drowned out by the increasing wind. The vessel lurched away from the dock, setting a course across the choppy channel between Faial and Pico. Rain pattered against the windows, blurring the view of the receding harbor.

Sandra's face paled as the boat pitched in the roughening seas. "I need to go topside for some fresh air," she managed, then hurried towards the stairs.

John exchanged a knowing look with Lauren, mouthing "sea sick" before following his wife to the upper deck.

Left alone, Lauren scanned the crowded ferry, her paranoia creeping in as she searched for any sign of Victor or his mysterious employer. The interior was a claustrophobic mix of locals and tourists, and their faces were obscured by rain jackets and the dim lighting.

A cheerful voice cut through her thoughts. "Beautiful day for a sea crossing, isn't it?" Lauren turned to find one of the Global Runners grinning at her with obvious sarcasm.

"Stacy, right?"

"Yes, exactly. We talked on the volcano run yesterday. That was a butt kicker. Up, up, up, and then down, down, down. I'm not used to that kind of terrain in Wisconsin." The woman sipped a hot cup of coffee, and Lauren's eyes tracked the movement.

"Where'd you get that?"

"Galley, or snack bar, whatever they call it." Then, she motioned for Lauren to follow her. "This way."

With the coffee situation settled, the two women settled into adjacent seats for the remainder of the trip.

Stacy asked, once they both got comfortable, "Where are you from? How do you like the Azores? What are you doing besides the official itinerary?" Clearly, the coffee made her even perkier than she normally seemed.

"I'm originally from North Carolina, but I've lived all over the place. Love the Azores so far. I think I could live here. And activities? I've kind of linked up with the Crismans. We go exploring when we're not on a run or the afternoon tourist thing," Lauren answered.

"So, what did you find on Faial that's interesting?"

Thinking about the question, Lauren filtered her answer so as not to trip into the treasure hunt. "Well, we checked out the Scrimshaw Museum. Very fascinating stuff there. Those sailors were genuine artists if they could carve those pictures into a whale's tooth." Then, looking at the other woman, she asked, "And what about your adventures?"

"Well, I love our outdoor activities. You don't get to run up a volcano in America. Besides those, I mostly focus on the people. I'm fascinated by what everyone does. I usually make a few good friends on these trips."

As they chatted, the ferry lurched into the harbor, the island's imposing volcano barely visible through the mist.

"Well, she didn't hurl, so that's a good thing," John announced as he helped Sandra down the metal steps.

"You don't have to tell them everything, John." Sandra may not have been sick, but she was clearly shaken by the voyage. Her complexion was whiter than usual, and her steps were unsteady.

"Global Runners! Everyone, this way to the buses," Susana called as she spotted members of their group. She effectively created a colorful parade of rain jackets and backpacks streaming towards waiting buses.

Their first stop was Arcos do Cachorro, a ghostly village of summer homes perched precariously on the island's rugged coast. The group followed concrete paths winding across natural lava arches, the angry Atlantic churning below.

Susana announced, "We're stopping here for pictures in the dog arches." She pointed toward a series of lava formations along the sea cliffs. There were multiple arches that had been the terminating points of lava tubes centuries before. The tourist bureau had created flat concrete walkways across the tops of the arches. Some were protected by handrails while others were totally open on both sides.

The group flowed down the path and out onto the rocks, snapping pictures in every direction as they went.

"Hey, look over here!" one runner shouted. He had found a lava sculpture of a dog sitting on a wall with its back to the sea. He was already posing for a selfie with his arm around the dog's neck.

John and Sandra walked confidently across the windswept formations, while Lauren trailed behind, acutely aware of Stacy's constant presence at her side. The roar of waves crashing against the cliffs nearly drowned out Susana's warnings about the treacherous waters.

"That's just beautiful," John said. Then, pointing beyond the rail, he added, "It seems the locals are brave enough to walk down and get in that water." There was a concrete path treacherously descending to the water's edge.

Susana chuckled. "Yes, if you live in the Azores, you're very comfortable swimming in the natural tide pools that are everywhere around the islands."

"And people don't drown in there?" John questioned.

"Oh, they do occasionally. It's usually a tourist, not a local, though."

Suddenly, a scream pierced the air, followed by a resounding splash. All eyes turned to see a figure thrashing in the churning waters below. It was Lauren, her head barely visible above the frothing waves.

Time seemed to slow as Susana sprang into action, her experience evident as she deftly tossed a life preserver to the struggling woman. Andrew emerged from the crowd and scrambled down the slippery path to the water's edge, ready to assist in any way he could.

After a harrowing few minutes, Lauren stood shivering on the lava shelf, her clothes plastered to her body, relief etched across her face. "Whew! That was a little terrifying," she managed between chattering teeth.

John rushed down to join them, and concern was etched in his voice when he said, "Lauren! Are you alright? What happened?"

Still catching her breath, Lauren gestured weakly towards the path above. "I was on the path up there. Then, I stumbled on something, and suddenly, I was falling."

As John followed her gaze, he saw Stacy among the group of onlookers, her face a mask of concern. But something in her stance, the way her hand gripped the rock wall, gave him pause. A flicker of suspicion crossed his mind as he turned back to Lauren, the implications of her near-disaster beginning to take shape in his thoughts.

CHAPTER 18

THE GUIDE

"Lauren, come with me. I have dry clothes that might fit you." Stacy had rushed to her new friend's side after she was fished out of the water and helped back up to the road.

"Really? That would be great. I wasn't planning on an ocean swim so early today." Lauren was still disoriented from her plummet into the sea. The water had been cool, but not cold. But the windy, cloudy weather was chilling her already wet skin. "The powerful waves in and out of that crevasse were the scariest part of the ordeal. I didn't know if I was going to be ground up against the sharp lava rocks or pulled out to sea. Luckily, I just sloshed back and forth like I was in a giant washing machine."

"Yes, luckily." Stacy took her arm and led her to the bus. She thrust a bundle of clothes towards her. "Here, you can change on the bus while everyone is still out there taking pictures." Stacy turned her back to give Lauren a little privacy.

As she pulled at her wet clothes, Lauren asked, "Did you see what happened? How did I fall off that walkway?"

"Sorry, I was right there behind you, but I was taking pictures in the other direction. I didn't know what was happening until I heard you scream. When I turned around, you were in midair, and then you splashed into the ocean."

"Hmm," was all Lauren said. She bundled her wet clothes into a ball and pushed them into a plastic shopping bag. Looking at her new dry outfit, she said, "These fit pretty well. Thanks. I'll get them back to you tonight at the hotel."

"Sure, no problem. It's not like you can run off with them." She chuckled at her own joke.

"Knock, knock." Sandra stuck her head in the bus door. "Is everyone decent in here?"

"I am now. Come on in." Lauren moved forward to meet her adventure partner.

"Lauren, if you're okay, John and I have an idea to discuss."

"Excuse me, Stacy. Business calls." Lauren hopped off the bus and hurried to where John was waiting.

John greeted her with a hug. "I'm so glad you're not hurt." Then he glanced over her shoulder at the bus. "But I'm wondering if your new friend had something to do with your accident."

Lauren's surprise was evident. "No, I don't think so. I just tripped on something."

John frowned. "If you say so. It just looked like she was standing awfully close to you when you fell. Then, she had a strange look on her face while she was standing on the rock and looking down at your situation. I don't think she was surprised or concerned."

"That's a lot to read into a quick glance." Lauren changed the subject. "What's this idea that Sandra mentioned?"

"Well, we're going to be in Madelana after this whaling museum. I've got the number for a mountain and trail guide there who might help us find the location in the scrimshaw images."

"Fine, I'm in. Let's do it."

"What's everyone talking about?" They all jumped, not expecting another person to speak, and turned to find Stacy smiling bright-eyed at all of them.

Sandra replied, "Whaling. That's the next event on the tour. Did you know they used to make vitamin pills from the whale bone they harvested?"

"Ick! No, I don't think I wanted to know that." Stacy wrinkled her nose at the idea.

～♪～♪～♪

The quaint coffee shop at the whaling museum buzzed with quiet conversation, its vintage decor evidence of Pico's rich maritime history. John settled onto a chrome-and-plastic chair, its familiar design evoking memories of childhood kitchens. The treasure hunters had discreetly slipped away from their tour group, anticipation building for their clandestine outing.

Sandra made the introductions with a flourish. "Everyone, this is Ricardo Silva. He's a trail and mountain guide. He can take us anywhere we want to go."

As John nodded a polite greeting, Lauren's gaze lingered on their new acquaintance. Ricardo cut an impressive figure. Tall and athletic, with sun-bronzed skin and eyes that sparkled with the allure of adventure, he fascinated her. His presence seemed to fill the small café and drew admiring glances from other patrons.

"*Bom dia.*" Ricardo's rich voice carried the musical lilt of the Azorean accent. "*Senhora* Crisman tells me you would like to explore the area around the volcano."

As John outlined their interest in the mountain, Lauren found herself captivated by the guide's confidence and the way his hands moved expressively as he spoke. When Ricardo revealed his knowledge of the Costa family, her face lit up with genuine excitement.

John offered more specific details. "We're trying to follow the history of Captain Costa. He served in the Portuguese Navy and was stationed here on the islands. Do you know of him?"

"Yes, of course. Everyone on the islands knows of the Costa family. They were very wealthy and important. There are many remnants of their work here. His family owned some cattle land on the side of the volcano."

"Maybe we should do some hikes on his cattle ranch. If that's possible, I mean," Lauren suggested as she leaned forward slightly, her eyes never leaving Ricardo's face.

Sandra was quick to add details. Pulling out her phone, she said, "We found beautiful scrimshaw carvings belonging to Costa. We'd like to visit some sites from these pictures." With the photo app open, she passed the phone to Richardo.

Ricardo's brow furrowed in concentration. His proximity to Lauren as he examined the phone sent a subtle thrill through her, the scent of sea salt and sun-warmed skin teasing her senses.

"These could be the west side of the mountain. That's where the old ranch was," Ricardo mused, his voice low and thoughtful. "There are still cattle on the land, but we are free to use the trails to climb to the top if we like."

Lauren seized the opportunity to engage him further. "Is there a Costa ranch house on those trails?"

Ricardo's eyes met hers, and a spark of shared enthusiasm seemed to pass between them. "Oh, yes, there was. It's just in ruins now, but I know where it is. It's close to one of the seldomly used trails."

"Can we start there?" Lauren asked.

"Of course. When would you like to go?"

John glanced at the others for confirmation. Then, he suggested, "Now?" Each of them nodded in agreement.

"Yes, I can take you now. I have a van outside we can use."

John informed Susana that his little group would be going on a private excursion. He also reassured her they would arrive at the hotel in Madelana by dinner time. Then, the group trouped out to the parking lot and got settled into Ricardo's van. Just as she was about to climb in, a flash of movement caught Lauren's eye.

Turning, she spotted Stacy standing outside the café they'd just left. The other woman appeared to be taking pictures of the van and their guide, which generated a quick flash of jealousy in Lauren's gut. Pushing the feeling aside, Lauren waved, receiving a casual acknowledgment in return.

As the van pulled away, Lauren settled into the passenger seat, acutely aware of Ricardo's presence next to her.

CHAPTER 19

IN THE FOG

The group passed through the lava-strewn ranch lands of Pico Island, leaving the quaint town behind. Verdant hillsides rolled out before them, a patchwork of lush vegetation, towering trees, and grazing cattle. Ricardo's voice filled the vehicle as he shared his knowledge of the island's flora.

"Most of that vegetation is not native to the Azores," he explained, gesturing at the passing landscape. "It was all brought here over the centuries and has flourished ever since."

Lauren, eager to engage their handsome guide once more, leaned forward in her seat. "What about the hibiscus that's all along the roads and trails?"

Ricardo's eyes met hers, showing a spark of appreciation for her curiosity. "Not even those. But they thrive so well here that they've almost become the national flower of the islands."

As they ascended the mountain, the weather transformed dramatically. The morning's wind and rain had given way to warm blue skies, only to be replaced by a thick, swirling fog that enveloped the mountain's base. The mist lent an air of mystery to their adventure, obscuring the road ahead.

They parked at the trailhead, where Ricardo shouldered his pack with practiced ease. "The trail starts here and heads up this face of the mountain. The old ranch house is on a flat spot up there in the fog. Is everyone ready?"

Each of his clients shouldered a small pack of their own and began following him up the narrow, barely visible path. The climb was a gentle slope, but it was also strewn with lava rocks of all sizes. Some were held in place by the aggressive vegetation. Others remained loose, threatening to roll underfoot. Ricardo led them with strong, confident strides through the obstacles. Lauren walked quickly to keep up with him while the Crismans trailed behind the pair in a more leisurely pace.

As they climbed, the road below them disappeared into the fog. They couldn't see the green pickup that had stopped on the road or the two figures who peered up, straining to keep the group in sight.

At a fork in the path, Ricardo paused. "You want to visit the house? It's down that way." He motioned to the left branch.

John nodded eagerly. "Yes, please. We'd like to see where the famous captain lived."

Lauren's gaze was drawn down the path, where she thought she glimpsed a figure moving away from them in the fog. "Hello?" she called out, pointing, but the apparition vanished as quickly as it had appeared.

Ricardo peered into the mist. "Olá. Is that Sebastian coming in the fog?"

John's head snapped up at the mention of the king whose treasure they were seeking. "What did you say?"

Ricardo chuckled. "It's an old Portuguese saying. When we meet someone walking through the fog, we say, 'Hello. Is that King Sebastian I see coming?' It refers to our most famous king. You may have heard of him?"

John replied, "Yes, we have heard of King Sebastian before. He's kind of the patron saint of the prosperous years of the Portuguese empire."

Ricardo's face brightened at his knowledge. "That's right. Legend says that Sebastian will return someday, emerging from the fog."

Lauren spoke up, eager to demonstrate her own knowledge of Portuguese history. She cited Sebastian's trip to Morocco to fight in the war and his subsequent disappearance. She decided not to mention the legend of the hidden gold treasure.

Attracted by her story, Ricardo filled in details that she hadn't included. Some were historical facts; others were legends that had emerged over the centuries. "You know," Ricardo added, his voice lowered conspiratorially, "many people believe King Sebastian hid gold from his treasury someplace in Portugal. There are no written records to substantiate that, but it hasn't stopped generations of people from scouring the country trying to find it."

Her heart racing at how close he was at guessing their true purpose behind this trip, Lauren feigned surprise. "Really? Do you believe the legends?"

Ricardo's hand came to rest on her shoulder, sending a warmth through her, despite the cool mist surrounding them. "In Portugal, we all believe in the legends of Sebastian. He represents the pinnacle of the empire and our hope for a prosperous future for the country. We believe there is a future when everyone in Portugal has everything they need, and we are a respected country in the world. But a literal chest of gold? No, we don't believe that it is just waiting to be found—and certainly not by anyone who is not Portuguese."

As they arrived at the stone fence surrounding the old ranch house, the fog parted momentarily, revealing the weathered walls of a traditional Portuguese dwelling. Two cows stood placidly beside the house, their presence adding a surreal touch to the misty scene.

While John and Sandra explored the house, Lauren's attention was drawn to the rugged slope behind it. "Is there a path back here? Maybe leading to a well or a garden?"

Ricardo nodded as his eyes scanned the terrain. "Yes, I think so. Around the other side and out the back. There is a fenced garden a little higher up."

Feeling the effects of the climb, Sandra sat down on the front steps of the house and announced, "We'll wait here. Give us a shout if you find anything worth seeing."

Lauren, eager to explore further, set off, with Ricardo close behind. As they rounded the house, stone steps materialized from the mist, leading upward to a faint trail. Lauren paused, once again glimpsing a shadowy figure in the fog.

"Hello, Sebastian," she called out playfully, glancing back at Ricardo with a mischievous smile. His warm chuckle echoed behind her as they pressed on, the mist swirling around them like a veil between the past and present, legend and reality.

CHAPTER 20

LURED ASTRAY

The fog hung heavy over the rugged terrain around the massive volcano, transforming the landscape into a ghostly realm of muted colors and indistinct shapes. Back on the narrow, winding road that snaked up the mountainside, a green pickup truck sat idle, its occupants peering intently into the mist that had swallowed their quarry.

Victor turned to his companion. "What do you want to do?" His voice was low, almost reverential, in the face of the ethereal scene before them.

Escobar scowled as he exited the truck. His movements were deliberate, each step accompanied by the soft tap of his ornate cane against the damp asphalt. "Follow them, obviously," he growled, his dark eyes glinting with determination.

Victor's gaze flickered to the cane, then back to the steep, treacherous path ahead. "It could be a tough climb," he warned.

Escobar's lips curled into a sardonic smile. "I can do it. This cane is mainly for beating idiots like you." With surprising agility for a man his age, he took the first steps into the dense underbrush that bordered the road. "Keep quiet," he hissed over his shoulder. "We don't want them to know we're here. This fog is a perfect cover for us."

As they entered the forest, the world around them seemed to close in. The mist clung to the gnarled branches of ancient trees, their bark slick with moisture. Ferns and moss carpeted the forest floor, muffled their footsteps, and added to the surreal atmosphere.

"How will we know where they went?" Victor whispered. His eyes darted nervously from shadow to shadow in the gloom.

Escobar's patience was wearing thin. Despite Victor's value as a connection to their target, the young man's constant questions grated on his nerves. "We follow the trail and keep our ears open," he explained tersely. "They think they're alone. So, they don't need to remain quiet, now do they?"

They paused, straining their ears to pick up the sounds of their targets. Sure enough, faint murmurs drifted down from somewhere above, barely audible over the soft patter of water droplets falling from leaf to leaf. With a shared nod of understanding, they began their ascent.

The climb was arduous, the path a treacherous mix of loose volcanic rock and slippery vegetation. Victor, with his athletic prowess, found the trail challenging but manageable. He moved with the grace of a predator, each step carefully placed, yet swift. Escobar, however, struggled against the limitations of his aging body. His breathing came in ragged gasps, and sweat beaded on his brow, despite the cool, damp air.

Their progress was frustratingly slow, with Victor constantly surging ahead, only to wait impatiently for Escobar to catch up. The fog seemed to thicken with each step, reducing visibility to a mere ten feet. Beyond that, the world dissolved into a swirling, opaque wall of gray.

Suddenly, Victor froze. "Oh, shit!" he hissed, his eyes wide with alarm. In the misty veil before him, a shadow had materialized—a vaguely human shape that seemed to drift rather than walk. His heart pounding, Victor's first thought was that they had inadvertently caught up to

Lauren's group. But then, he heard voices coming from higher up the mountain, unmistakably distant.

He looked again, and there it was—the shadow, moving away from him with an otherworldly grace. A chill that had nothing to do with the damp air ran down his spine.

Backtracking down the trail, Victor moved close to Escobar, his voice barely above a whisper. "I think there's someone else on the trail. I just saw them in the mist, but Lauren and her group are much higher." He pointed toward the distant voices, his hand trembling slightly as he did so.

Escobar's brow furrowed as he considered this unexpected development. The notion that anyone else would be out in this remote area seemed absurd, let alone on the very same trail between them and their target. "It had to be a tree or just a clear spot in the fog," he reasoned, but it sounded as if it was more to convince himself than Victor.

"It looked like it was walking away from us," Victor insisted.

Exasperation flashed across Escobar's face. "Well, then, run ahead and catch them," he snapped. "Find out who it is, and tell them to bugger off."

Victor hesitated and searched Escobar's face for any sign that he was joking. Finding none, he nodded reluctantly.

"Okay, I'll be right back." With those words, he bounded up the trail, his powerful legs propelling him forward at a breakneck pace.

Left alone, Escobar resumed his steady, methodical climb. The tap of his cane against stone and the rasp of his labored breathing were the only sounds he could hear in the eerie stillness of the fog-shrouded forest.

Victor, in his haste to catch the mysterious figure, failed to notice the fork in the trail that led to the old cabin. His eyes strained against the mist, searching desperately for any sign of movement. The world around him had taken on a dreamlike quality, with twisted tree trunks looming out of the fog like silent sentinels and shadows flickering at the edges of his vision.

Minutes passed, and still, Victor pressed on, unaware that he had passed his intended quarry. The voices he had heard earlier had faded away, replaced by an oppressive silence broken only by the hammering rhythm of his own heart.

Escobar, meanwhile, had just reached the fork in the trail himself. Without hesitation, he continued up the main path, his singular focus on catching up to Lauren's group blinding him to the possibility that they might have taken the side trail. Soon, both men had unwittingly bypassed their targets and were venturing deeper into the wilderness, alone and increasingly lost.

As they pushed further into the mist-shrouded unknown, neither man noticed the subtle shift in the surrounding air. The fog seemed to thicken, taking on an almost sentient quality. Somewhere in the depths of that ethereal veil, a shadow moved with purpose, leading them further astray with each step.

CHAPTER 21

FINALLY CLOSE

Lauren rushed up the trail behind the cabin. She was checking every tree and every cliff to match them with the pictures they had taken.

Ricardo trailed slightly behind her. "You seem determined to find something specific here. What are you looking for?"

"I thought Captain Costa might have carved the images from his back garden. Maybe the scene on the scrimshaw is around here someplace. I'd like to have a picture of the scrimshaw and a matching picture of the actual place."

"Tourists," Ricardo muttered under his breath. Aloud, he said, "Show me the image again, and I'll help you look for it." He stared intently at the screen of the phone that Lauren held up for his inspection.

"I think the cliffs should look about the same, even after all these years, but the trees are probably different. Maybe there are more of them, or maybe they're all dead." Still, she didn't give up and continued to examine every cliff face she could get to.

Finally, they arrived at the flat space where Ricardo said the Costa family had kept a garden. It was covered with a layer of soil that seemed out of place for the terrain they were in. She turned to her guide. "Where did they get this soil? It doesn't look native to this area."

Ricardo smiled. "You're very observant. That soil is from Faial Island. This island is so new that soil hasn't had time to accumulate. But a couple of centuries ago, the locals discovered they could grow grapes here on the lava, if they brought in soil. So, they imported boat after boat full of soil from Faial. Some was purchased, some was just taken. That's how they created all the vineyards around the island. It's also the basis for every garden here."

Lauren just said, "Interesting," and returned to examining the cliff face. She realized the origins of soil didn't contribute to her search for a specific location. Then, after taking a second and closer look at the surrounding landscape, she approached a cliff that seemed to have the same dimensions as the one in the scrimshaw. In front of it grew two trees with the rotted stump of a third nearby. "This one looks close."

"Maybe," conceded Ricardo. He showed little interest in this photo excursion, as he didn't much see the point of it. However, his interest in Lauren encouraged him to put more enthusiasm into this search than he otherwise would have.

As Lauren clambered over loose lava rocks to get a closer look at the cliff face, one rock rolled under her feet, and she tipped backward, about to tumble into the rocky forest behind her. In an instant, she felt an iron grip around her forearm and another firm hand behind her back. Ricardo snatched her mid-fall and pulled her upright next to him.

"Yikes, that was a close one," Lauren said as she grasped both of Ricardo's arms. She smiled up at him and, for the first time, was close enough to see the dark speckles in his eyes. Scenes from multiple movies flashed through her mind. This moment would be where the two lovers exchanged their first kiss, alone in the forest. And as fast as the image appeared, she pushed it away, thinking to herself, *That's what happens in the movies, not real life.*

"You're okay. I got you." He held her by the elbows and looked into her hazel eyes. Ricardo's mind didn't replay scenes from a movie. Instead, he pulled her in close and gently placed his lips against hers. Then, he drew back a few centimeters to gauge her reaction. Her face said everything he needed to know. He returned for another kiss, one with more meaning behind it. They both stood in the embrace for several moments, savoring the heat that was building between them.

Lauren thought, *Maybe I am in a movie.*

From below, they heard Sandra's voice calling up to them. "Have you found anything?"

Lauren said in a whisper, "Oh, yes, definitely. I've found something." Then, in a louder voice, she replied, "Nothing yet. I'll let you know if you should come up."

Lauren and Ricardo both smiled at each other. Then he asked, "Are you still interested in that cliff scene?"

The question snapped Lauren's mind back to her mission, back to the quest for gold. She released her grip on him and answered, "Well, for now, yes, I'm still looking for it. But I'm thinking of focusing on something different later."

"I can wait until later," he said.

Returning her attention to the cliff, she examined the face until she found a spot that seemed to have been cleared flat for a carving. The crevasses were filled with moss and gravel. She brushed at them with the sleeve of her jacket. With each pass, an image gradually emerged.

Finally, once it was almost fully exposed, she stepped back, pointed at the surface, and asked, "What does that look like to you?"

Ricardo leaned forward, intentionally bringing his face close to Lauren's. He could feel the heat from her cheek. Returning his attention to the rock, he said, "It's a circle with something inside it."

Lauren held up a fist and slipped her thumb between her index and middle finger. She asked, "Like this?"

Ricardo blinked in recognition. "A *figa*? Yes, it could be that."

Lauren called down the mountain, "Sandra, I think you'd better come and look at this."

John and Sandra both rose to their feet and started up the trail, but they weren't the only ones who'd heard Lauren's call. Two figures who had been wandering in the mists turned around and started back down the slope.

CHAPTER 22

FOUND

The world around them seemed to be frozen in time as John and Sandra stared at the symbol etched into the ancient cliff face. The *figa*, weathered by centuries of wind and rain, stood out starkly against the dark basalt.

"I don't believe it," John murmured, his voice barely above a whisper.

Sandra held her phone up, capturing the image for later study. "It's just like the carving on the whale's tooth," she said, and her voice trembled with excitement. Her gaze shifted to the surrounding vegetation. "These trees are newer and in different positions. They must be the descendants that grew from fallen seeds."

Ricardo, standing slightly apart from the group, watched their reactions with growing curiosity. Unable to contain himself any longer, he interjected, "It's just ancient graffiti. People carve their initials in rocks all the time."

Lauren gently placed her hand on his arm, her touch electric against his skin. "But this one was important enough that Costa captured it in a scrimshaw that he valued. Why would he do that?" As she spoke, a realization dawned on her. They would have to trust Ricardo with at least part of their secret if they wanted his valuable insight into Pico's terrain and history. He had been helpful so far, but without knowing their plan, he wouldn't know how to help them. She glanced at the Crismans, silently urging them to come to the same conclusion.

John turned to face their guide, his expression a mixture of caution and resolve. "Ricardo, we're searching for more than just the history of Captain Costa. He may have held valuable artifacts somewhere here on the island. We hope to recover those if we can."

Ricardo's eyebrows lifted in surprise. "What kind of artifacts? Like nautical sextants or compasses?"

"Hopefully, those kinds of things," John replied in an effort to carefully choose his words. "We'll know if we find them." He gestured towards the *figa*. "This symbol has been a guide throughout our search thus far." The unspoken weight of their true quest hung in the air between them.

Lauren, meanwhile, had been scrutinizing the cliff wall. Her fingers traced the rough surface as she spoke. "Clearly, it isn't embedded in this lava wall. It's just solid basalt here. It hasn't been broken up since whatever eruption deposited it thousands of years ago."

Sandra, ever the practical one, extracted a small folding shovel from her pack. "I'm going to poke around in that garden soil. I don't know where else to start."

As Sandra began her methodical exploration, Lauren turned to Ricardo. "Are we at the end of this little trail, or does it go on?"

Ricardo pointed to their left, where the vegetation grew thick and wild. "There's no more trail, but you can see the flat area continues in that direction. It's almost completely blocked by trees."

Determination flashed in Lauren's eyes. "Then let's keep looking that way." She stepped gingerly over the loose lava rocks, her boots crunching on the uneven surface. Squeezing between the gnarled trunks of ancient trees, she called back, "It doesn't look like a trail. But it is flat enough, so I'm going to keep going."

His voice firm with resolve, Ricardo said, "I'm coming with you."

Lauren pushed through the dense foliage, which caused branches to scrape against her face and arms. Suddenly, the ground beneath her feet gave way. With a startled cry of "Aiee!" she dropped two feet into a hidden depression.

Ricardo was at her side in an instant, his firm hand grasping hers and pulling her to a sitting position. Lauren found herself perched at the edge of a dark opening, her legs dangling into the void below.

"What is that?" she asked with a gasp, and she could feel her heart racing. "I almost broke my leg."

Ricardo leaned forward to peer into the inky blackness. His eyes widened with recognition. "It's a lava tube," he said in a voice tinged with excitement.

Seeing Lauren's puzzled expression, he launched into an explanation. "When a volcano erupts and lava flows across the surface, the upper layer of the flow is exposed to colder air. The top eventually cools and hardens into a shell. But inside, the molten lava keeps flowing. It's like oil in a pipeline. Eventually, the eruption stops and the lava runs out the far end. When the last of the molten material has flowed down a slope into the sea or onto a flat plane, the pipe is empty, but the shell is still there. The shell is always two or three meters thick and right near the surface. Just like this one."

Lauren listened intently. All the while, her mind raced with possibilities. "These are common on the island?"

Ricardo nodded enthusiastically. "Oh, yes, we have hundreds of them. Inside, they're all about the same. The hollow tube is two to four meters high and empty. Some of these are close enough to roads that we take tourists through them." He paused, his gaze drawn back to the mysterious opening. "This one, no one has probably seen in generations. Maybe not even since the Costa family left."

Lauren's excitement built as she absorbed the information. To her, this lava tube sounded like the perfect hiding place for something priceless. "When was this one formed?"

Ricardo furrowed his brow, considering the question. "I don't know for sure. Here on the west side of the island, there have been no lava flows for 1,000 years. So, this one must be really old."

Lauren's eyes gleamed with determination as she asked the question that burned in her mind: "Can we look inside?"

The hidden entrance to the lava tube yawned before them, a portal to the island's ancient past. The mist seemed to swirl around them, as if nature itself was holding its breath in anticipation of what they might discover in the depths below.

Ricardo produced headlamps from his pack and handed one to her. "A guide has to be prepared," he explained. "Just watch your step. The edges can be sharp."

Once inside, Lauren looked left and right. The tube appeared to lie directly under the path they'd been exploring. Taking deep breaths, Lauren asked, "Why is the air in here so fresh? It's not stuffy or sulfurous."

"This volcano has been dormant for 1,000 years. There are probably several more holes in this tube for the wind to blow through."

Then, a thought occurred to Lauren that caused her knees to feel weak. "Bats?"

Chuckling, Ricardo said, "No bats. They can't echolocate in the porous lava, so it's dangerous for them to fly in here."

Lauren started walking uphill inside the tube. The footing available to her was more treacherous than what they had encountered above, as lava rocks of all sizes made up the floor of the tube.

Ricardo reached out and grasped her hand. "For safety," he said with a smile. Lauren happily accepted his warm hand and firm grip. Together, they proceeded cautiously, their headlamps exposing the inner features of the tube for the first time in centuries.

"What are we looking for?" Ricardo finally asked.

"I'm pretty sure it's that." Lauren pointed ahead of them on the floor. There was a dark object with flecks of light reflected from their headlamps.

"A brass instrument?"

Lauren's heart pounded with excitement. In the darkness, she smiled at her companion's innocence. "Let's see," she replied as they approached the object and the full-strength of both headlamps concentrated on it.

They stood next to a single, wooden chest bound with iron bands. It was smaller than Lauren expected. The wood was badly rotted, the iron rusted and brittle, but yellow light shown from cracks in its surface. Lauren laid a hand on the top, seeking a lid. The wood crumbled into dust and splinters at her touch. She reached straight through the material and grasped the internal contents. Her hand came away black with decaying material, and she brushed the dirt away to reveal a gleaming, golden circle in her palm.

"Gold!" Ricardo exclaimed. "It's a chest of gold coins!"

"Exactly what we've been looking for," Lauren confirmed. Turning the coin over in her hand, she could see a crown on one side and a *figa* symbol on the other. "The lost treasure of King Sebastian."

Lauren and Ricardo stood in stunned silence for a moment, the weight of their discovery settling over them like a blanket of golden light. Suddenly, Lauren let out a joyous whoop that filled the ancient lava tube, startling them both before they dissolved into laughter.

"We did it!" she cried, her face beaming with excitement. "We actually found it!"

Ricardo's expression morphed from shock to elation as the reality of their discovery sank in. He grabbed Lauren's hands, the coin still clutched between them, and spun her around in a spontaneous dance of celebration. Their laughter bounced off the walls of the tube, filling the space with the sound of pure, unbridled joy.

"I can't believe it!" Ricardo exclaimed, and his eyes were wide with wonder. "In all my years of guiding, I never imagined I'd be part of something like this!"

Lauren held the coin up, watching it gleam in the light of their headlamps. "Just think of the history we're holding," she marveled. "These coins have been waiting here for centuries, carrying the legacy of King Sebastian and the dreams of Captain Costa." Then, she offered the coin to him. "This one is a gift from me to you. It is not treasure to be sold." Ricardo accepted it with a smile and slipped it into his pocket.

Their excitement was infectious. They hugged tightly, caught up in the moment of shared triumph, which led to them kissing in this dark place of mystery. As they pulled apart, both slightly breathless, their eyes met with a new understanding—they were now bound by this extraordinary secret.

"We have to show John and Sandra!" Lauren suddenly remembered.

Ricardo nodded enthusiastically. "Yes, and we need to figure out how to get this treasure out safely. This is going to change everything!"

As their initial burst of celebration subsided, a more serious realization settled over them. They exchanged a knowing look, acknowledging the enormous responsibility that now rested on their shoulders.

Lauren took a deep breath, centering herself. "You're right, we can't carry it out in that chest," she said. Her mind was already busy with trying to come up with potential solutions.

Ricardo replied by shrugging off his pack and emptying the contents onto the ground. "Let's see how much we can carry in these."

As they began the careful process of transferring the coins, the air in the lava tube seemed to hum with possibility. The darkness that had shrouded this treasure for so long was pierced not just by their headlamps, but by the bright promise of the future they had just uncovered. Every coin they placed in their packs was a piece of history, a fragment of a long-lost dream finally brought to light.

The excitement of their discovery mingled with a sense of reverence for the moment. They were not just treasure hunters now, but guardians of a secret that had waited centuries to be revealed. As they worked, Lauren and

Ricardo shared glances filled with a mix of exhilaration and the weight of their newfound responsibility.

The lava tube, which had been silent for so long, now resonated with the quiet sounds of their careful work and the occasional whisper of awe as they uncovered more of the beautiful coins. The musty scent of the ages-old wood mingled with the metallic tang of the gold, creating an olfactory memory they would never forget.

As they finished filling their packs, the reality of their situation truly sank in. They were about to emerge from this ancient volcanic vein with a treasure that would rewrite history books and change their lives forever. The darkness of the lava tube seemed to press in around them, as if reluctant to let go of its long-held secret.

CHAPTER 23

LOST

The Azores sun blazed triumphantly as Lauren and Ricardo emerged from the lava tube, its warmth a stark contrast to the cool darkness they'd left behind. The fog had lifted and revealed a sky so blue that it seemed to mock their earlier struggles. Their packs, heavy with golden treasure, weighed on their shoulders but lifted their spirits to dizzying heights.

"Can you believe it? We actually found it! John and Sandra will be astounded," Lauren said as she stepped carefully between the trees on the path.

Ricardo nodded and beamed, a grin filled with a mixture of pride and disbelief. "It's like a dream," he said before adjusting his pack. "A very heavy dream."

As they made their way back to the garden clearing, their elation was palpable. Every step felt lighter, despite the weight they carried. The world seemed brighter, more vivid, as if the discovery had sharpened their senses.

They found John and Sandra in the clearing, exhausted and grimy from their fruitless search of the garden. The contrast between their dejected postures and Lauren and Ricardo's triumphant return couldn't have been more clear.

"I see you have both been hard at work. Any luck?" asked Lauren.

Sandra shook her head. "Nothing valuable. Some broken pottery and animal bones. And a few potatoes are actually growing in there." She pointed to a filthy pile of their discoveries. "How about you?"

Both Lauren and Ricardo broke into huge smiles. Dropping her pack to the ground, Lauren said, "Nothing much." Then, she reached inside and extracted one gold coin and held it up for the others to see. "Just this." She kicked the pack so they could hear the clink of metal inside. Ricardo followed suit by dropping his pack next to hers with the heavy clinking of coins declaring its contents.

The transformation in John and Sandra was instantaneous. Their fatigue evaporated, replaced by a surge of unbridled joy. John's hands trembled as he examined the coin for himself, his eyes wide with wonder.

"We did it," Sandra whispered, her voice thick with emotion. "We really did it."

The sense of elation that shot through John and Sandra's bodies was beyond anything they had ever experienced before. They both felt more energized and alive than they had in decades. Even finding a single coin would have overshadowed all of their previous discoveries, but an entire bag of the coins was more than they could even imagine.

Their moment of triumph was brutally short-lived. Victor's voice, dripping with smug satisfaction, shattered their celebration like a stone through glass. "So good of you to do all the work for us, honey."

Lauren's heart plummeted, causing her elation to curdle into a sickening mix of rage and betrayal. Victor's leering face, once familiar and beloved, now seemed grotesque with greed as he and his new friend walked toward them.

"Victor, you bastard!" she spat.

The scene unfolded like a nightmare. Victor, gloating and triumphant. The stranger, Escobar, cold and menacing with his pistol. And Ricardo, silent and tense, recognizing the grave danger they were in.

As Victor scooped up the coins, each clink felt like a physical blow to Lauren. Their dream, so briefly held, was slipping through their fingers like sand.

Looking at Lauren, John asked, "Friends of yours?"

Almost spitting, Lauren replied, "Just my bastard of an ex-boyfriend. And I don't know who his new boss is."

Ricardo remained silent during the entire exchange. He didn't know the ex-boyfriend, but he certainly knew who the older man was. Duarte Escobar was renowned on the islands for his shady business deals and his ruthless treatment of those who crossed him. Ricardo knew that they probably wouldn't survive this confrontation.

Escobar spoke for the first time. Pointing to Ricardo, he said, "He knows who I am." Ricardo nodded slightly. Then, turning to his partner, Escobar snapped, "Victor, you shoulder that pack." To Ricardo, he said, "And you pick yours up again. You're coming with us." Both men did as they were ordered.

Lauren felt as if the ground had dropped out from under her. The fear that gripped her was visceral, an icy fist squeezing her heart. "No!" she cried, her voice raw with desperation. "You can't take him!"

Escobar replied, "He's a local, but you three are Americans. I don't want trouble with your government. You can do whatever you want. Somehow, however, I do not believe that you'll tell the authorities you came here to steal Portugal's historical treasures."

They watched helplessly as Victor roughly grabbed Ricardo. In that moment, Lauren saw his fear, but also his determination to shield them from harm.

As Escobar and Victor left with Ricardo and the treasure, Lauren felt a maelstrom of emotions. The crushing disappointment of losing the gold warred with her terror for Ricardo's safety. She wanted to run after them, to fight, to do something, anything. But the cold reality of Escobar's gun kept her rooted to the spot.

"What will you do with Ricardo?" she called out, her voice cracking with fear and frustration.

Escobar's disdainful silence was more chilling than any threat. As they disappeared down the trail, Lauren felt as if a part of her was being torn away. The beautiful day now seemed to mock them, the bright sun illuminating the bitter depths of their loss.

In the oppressive silence of the clearing, Lauren, John, and Sandra stood shellshocked. Their greatest triumph had turned to ashes in their mouths, leaving behind only the rancid taste of defeat and the gnawing fear for Ricardo's life.

CHAPTER 24

FAMILY CONNECTIONS

Lauren stood at the edge of the clearing with her eyes fixed on the spot where Ricardo, Victor, and Escobar had disappeared down the mountain trail. The weight of their loss pressed down on her, as tangible as the treasure they'd so briefly held.

Sandra's voice, tight with frustration, broke the oppressive silence. "I don't even know who to call. We can't exactly report stolen gold coins to the authorities, can we?" She ran her fingers through her hair, leaving streaks of dirt across her forehead.

John nodded grimly, and his usually jovial face was etched with concern. "And something tells me this Escobar character isn't just some common thug. He's got that air about him, you know? The kind of man who probably has half the island in his pocket."

Lauren paced back and forth, her movements sharp and agitated. Replaying the events of the past hour over and over in her mind, she couldn't seem to focus on anything else besides the elation of their discovery, the shock of Victor's betrayal, and now the gnawing fear for Ricardo's safety. She stopped abruptly, turning to face John and Sandra.

"What about Ricardo? We can't just leave him with those monsters. God knows what they might do to him." She took a step towards the trail, her body coiled with tension. "Should we follow them?"

John and Sandra exchanged a worried glance. The dilemma was clear on their faces—the desire to help warring with the genuine danger of the situation.

"Lauren," John began, his tone gentle but firm, "I know you're worried about Ricardo. We all are. But we have to be smart about this. We can't just charge blindly after them."

Lauren opened her mouth to argue, but before she could utter a word, a sharp crack split the air. The sound of a gunshot echoed off the mountainside.

Time seemed to stand still for a heartbeat, then felt like it was moving as fast as the speed of light. "Oh, my God!" Lauren screamed, her voice raw with terror. Without a backward glance, she bolted down the trail, her feet barely touching the ground.

"Lauren, wait!" John called after her, but his words were lost in the rush of wind and the pounding of her own heart in her ears.

Lauren ran as she'd never run before. The trail that had taken them nearly an hour to climb now flew by in a blur of green and brown. Branches whipped at her face and arms, but she barely felt the sting.

As she neared the bottom of the trail, the sound of an engine revving and tires crunching on gravel reached her ears. The noise grew fainter with each passing second, spurring her to even greater speed.

She burst out of the tree line onto the road, her eyes wildly scanning the area. For a moment, her heart stopped as she spotted a figure slumped against Ricardo's van.

"Ricardo!" she cried out. Her voice cracked with emotion halfway through his name. She sprinted towards him, praying to whatever gods might be listening that he was still alive.

At the sound of her voice, Ricardo's head snapped up, his eyes wide with surprise. "Lauren?" he called back, and the confusion he felt was clear in his tone. He stood up as she approached.

Relief flooded through her like a tidal wave as she reached him. She grasped his arms as her eyes frantically searched for any sign of injury. "Where are you shot? Lay down, you shouldn't be standing up!"

Ricardo's puzzled expression slowly morphed into understanding. He gently took her hands in his, his touch warm and reassuring. "I'm fine," he whispered, a small smile playing at the corners of his mouth. He stepped aside to reveal the van's flat tire. "He shot the tire, the bastard."

The tension drained from Lauren's body so quickly that she felt lightheaded. She stared at the flat tire, then back at Ricardo, then at the tire again. A confusing mix of relief and frustration welled up inside her, culminating in a strangled laugh that was half of a sob. Tears streamed down her face as she punched Ricardo's arm, not entirely gently. "You scared the shit out of me!"

Ricardo winced at the punch, but his smile only grew wider. Without a word, he pulled her into a tight embrace. Lauren melted into his arms, the adrenaline of the past few minutes finally catching up with her. She could feel Ricardo's heart pounding against her cheek, a tangible reminder that he was here, alive and whole.

They stood like that for what felt like an eternity, drawing comfort from each other's presence. The sound of labored breathing broke the moment, and they turned to see John and Sandra emerging from the trail, both red-faced and breathing heavily.

"Thank goodness," Sandra gasped between breaths, leaning heavily on John. "When we heard that shot, we feared the worst."

John nodded, still too winded to speak. His eyes, however, spoke volumes as they darted between Lauren and Ricardo.

As they caught their breath, Ricardo explained what had transpired after he'd been taken. His voice was calm, but Lauren could detect an undercurrent of tension as he spoke.

"As we walked down the trail, Escobar and I had a… conversation," Ricardo said, his brow furrowing slightly. "I told him about my family, about growing up here. It turns out my mother is related to him—some kind of in-law connection."

Lauren's eyes widened in surprise. "That's…I don't even know if that's terrible or wonderful."

Ricardo's smile was tinged with a hint of bitterness. "It means he knows I can't turn him in to the authorities. Where would I hide? What would happen to my family?" He shook his head, a resigned look settling over his features. "It's a delicate balance we all live with here on the island."

Lauren felt a pang of guilt at his plight. "Oh, Ricardo, I'm so sorry. We never meant to put your family in danger."

Ricardo waved away her concern, but his eyes softened as they met hers. "It's not your fault, Lauren. As I said, it's nothing new. We've lived under Escobar's shadow for years."

A moment of silence fell over the group as they absorbed this new information. The complexity of island life, with its web of family connections and unspoken rules, was becoming clearer—and more daunting.

John broke the silence. "I don't want to seem cold, but we need to figure out how to get back to town. We can't exactly call a taxi out here."

Ricardo looked the group up and down, his gaze lingering on their footwear. A slow smile spread across his face. "A guide has to be prepared for anything," he said before reaching into the van and pulling out four bottles of water. He distributed them to everyone. "We're dressed for a run. So, let's run back."

Lauren glanced longingly back up the mountain trail, remembering the treasure that had so recently slipped through their fingers. For a moment, she was tempted to suggest they return to the cave, but she knew this wasn't the time for that. Their priority now had to be getting back to civilization and figuring out their next move.

As they set off at an easy pace down the road, Lauren fell into step beside Ricardo. The rhythmic sound of their footfalls on the dusty surface was oddly comforting.

Despite the loss of the treasure and the danger they'd faced, she felt a strange sense of excitement building within her.

This setback, she realized, was just that—a setback. Their adventure wasn't over; it had merely taken an unexpected turn. As they ran, Lauren thought of what would come next. *How can we reclaim what is rightfully ours? How will we navigate the treacherous waters of island politics and family loyalties?*

The sun beat down on their backs as they ran, a constant reminder of the golden prize they'd briefly held. In the steady rhythm of their synchronized steps, a new resolve was forming. Today was not the end of their quest, but merely the beginning of a new chapter.

CHAPTER 25

AFTERMATH AND BEGINNINGS

The sun dipped towards the horizon as Ricardo led the small group back to their resort. The rocky shore of Pico Island stretched out before them, a stark contrast to the verdant mountainside they had left behind. The ocean between Pico and Faial churned restlessly, its waves crashing against the volcanic rock barriers that served as a makeshift beach.

Lauren's legs ached from the unexpected run, but her mind was racing even faster than her feet had been. Losing the treasure still stung, but a spark of determination had ignited within her. She watched Ricardo's back as he walked ahead, his posture tense but purposeful. Despite everything, she felt a flutter in her stomach that had nothing to do with the exhaustion she felt.

As they stepped through the hotel's ornate doors, the cool, air-conditioned breeze was a welcome respite. Sheryl, the ever-cheerful event director from Global Runners, greeted them with a mix of relief and curiosity. "Where have you all been? We were about to send out a search party. It seems you've had quite the adventure this afternoon."

John, as they had hastily agreed, took the lead. His voice was steady, but Lauren could detect a hint of strain as he spun their cover story. "Ricardo here took us on a private exploration of the volcano. We wanted to get up the face 1,000 feet or so."

Sheryl glanced at her watch, and her brow furrowed in confusion. "But you all left nearly six hours ago. That's quite the hike."

John attempted a rueful smile, though the expression did not quite reach his eyes. "Bad luck, I'm afraid. When we came down the mountain, Ricardo's van had a flat tire—and no spare. So, being the outdoorsy types we are, we decided to run back here." He glanced at his GPS watch, as if to confirm. "Just over ten kilometers, but we made it."

Sheryl chuckled, satisfied with the explanation. "You're exactly the kind of adventurers we love to see on these trips. Dinner will be in an hour. Your guide is welcome to join us, of course."

As Lauren and Sandra dispersed to mingle with other group members, weaving a tapestry of truths and fabrications about their day, Ricardo's attention was caught by a familiar face in the parking lot. A woman was loading racing supplies into a car, her movements efficient and practiced.

"Susana, *bom dia*!" Ricardo called out, excited at the sight of his former high school classmate.

Susana's face lit up with recognition. "Ricardo, so good to see you." She nodded towards the lobby. "How did my runners fare on the mountain?"

Ricardo felt a weight lift from his shoulders. Here was someone he could trust, someone who understood the delicate balance of island life. "They were solid. Even agreed to run back here when we had a flat tire." He paused, lowering his voice when he revealed, "But we did have a little trouble up there."

Susana's eyebrows shot up. "Oh? Weather?"

Ricardo shook his head, his voice now dropping to a near whisper. "Duarte Escobar."

Susana inhaled sharply and immediately understood the gravity of the situation. "And?"

"He didn't take kindly to us hiking around the old Costa ranch cabin. You know it?" Ricardo's tone was casual, but his eyes were filled with intent.

Susana's brow furrowed in confusion. "Why? Who would care about that pile of rocks?"

"Exactly," Ricardo replied, his mind working furiously to figure out the answer as to why Escobar was there in the first place. *Did someone tip him off? They had to have, but who?* "Now, I think I owe him an apology. Do you know where he's staying on the island?"

Susana considered for a moment. "He has a place in Baixo facing the ocean. It's the one on the main road with whale sculptures for gate handles. You can't miss it."

Ricardo nodded, committing the information to memory. "Thanks. Oh, and Sheryl invited me to stay for dinner."

"Good!" Susana smiled and pointed to a picturesque restaurant with its own dock jutting out into the ocean. "We're eating just there on the waterfront." She paused, then added, "You know, tomorrow night, the group is doing a wine tasting and dinner at *Senhor* Escobar's vineyard. He might be there for the party."

Ricardo felt a jolt of excitement and fear. This information was the kind they needed to formulate a plan. He thanked Susana and made his way back to the hotel.

As he entered the lobby, his eyes immediately sought Lauren. She was laughing with a group of runners, but he could see the tension in her shoulders, the slight strain around her eyes. Their gazes met across the room, and a silent understanding passed between them.

Later, as the group made their way to the waterfront restaurant, Ricardo fell into step beside her. The setting sun painted the sky in breathtaking hues of orange and pink, reflecting off the restless ocean waves.

"I have some information," he murmured, keeping his voice low. "About Escobar and his whereabouts."

Lauren's eyes widened, and a mix of apprehension and excitement flickering across her face. "That's…good, right?" she whispered back.

Ricardo nodded, a small smile playing at the corners of his mouth. "It's a start. We'll talk more after dinner. But Lauren," he paused, his expression growing serious, "whatever we do next, it's going to be dangerous. Are you sure you want to pursue this?"

Lauren glanced ahead at John and Sandra, then back at Ricardo. The fading sunlight caught in her eyes, where determination shined brightly. "I'm sure," she said firmly. "We've come too far to give up now."

As they reached the restaurant, the aroma of grilled seafood and the sound of laughter filled the air. But beneath the jovial atmosphere, a current of anticipation thrummed between Lauren and Ricardo. The evening ahead promised good food and company, but more importantly, it offered the chance to plan, to strategize, to hope.

ALONE WITH FEARS

The sumptuous dinner by the sea had been a stark contrast to the day's harrowing events. As night fell, the four adventurers went their separate ways, each grappling with the aftermath of their encounter with Escobar.

John sat in a chair turned toward the glass sliding door. He stared out of it to see street lights reflecting faintly off the chapel behind the hotel. The darkness outside mirrored the tumultuous thoughts swirling in his mind.

Treasure hunting is supposed to be a fun hobby, not a life-threatening terror. I've never actually met anyone like Escobar before. Men like him have always been fictional characters on the screen. The gun he held was real, though. He could have shot any of us and just walked away. We were defenseless. Reasoning and pleading with him might not have worked at all if he had stuck around much longer.

What's more important, adventure or life? Entertainment or Sandra? I had no right to put her in danger. Life without her would be so empty. What if he'd just shot me? How would she carry on? Would it break her emotionally? Mentally?

On the bed, Sandra pretended to read a book about Portuguese history, occasionally glancing over at John's rigid silhouette. The page before her showed the massive volcano, triggering a flood of memories and conflicting emotions.

Gold. What are we going to do with a pack full of gold if we manage to get it all back, anyway? We're too old to change our lifestyle, even if we had a million dollars. How much is half of that stash worth? I don't even know. A million? Two? More? Does it matter? The point isn't the money, it's the adventure. It's the thrill. It's the act of searching, finding clues, solving puzzles. Escobar doesn't care about adventure; he just cares about the money. He'll probably melt the coins down to make them easier to sell. Whatever history they carry will be lost forever.

I don't think he would have shot us. Too messy. Americans killed in a foreign country would be too risky. Even a mob boss can't fight against an American investigation. He was in more danger than we were. What if we had resisted? What could he have done, really? Oh, well, maybe Ricardo would have been his target? Well, that's not what happened. Now, the gold is gone. Is John heartbroken? Lauren is probably near a mental breakdown. Anyone could see she's taken to Ricardo. Tomorrow, we'll get back in sync with Global Runners. We'll do their events, drink some wine, and behave like regular tourists. Gold? Who cares?

Several rooms down the hall, Lauren lay back on her own bed. It was dark. Her roommate was sound asleep. She wished sleep would take her as well, but the day had been too intense. Her mind kept her awake with thoughts of what-ifs and what steps they needed to take next.

Would Escobar have shot Ricardo? Killed him? It's not like we're in love. We barely know each other. Sure, we shared a kiss…or two. But that's all. Probably not going any further once we get our treasure back. That's our gold. That's our future. Well, my future. Escobar is just going to build an evil empire with it. Probably make things worse for the people on the islands. Taking it away from him would be better for everyone. He thinks we're afraid of him. Well…because we are. Would he kill an American? Probably, but only as a last resort. That doesn't mean we do nothing, not when that gold is rightfully ours. We have to do something to get it back. Ricardo has to disappear. We can't involve him. Escobar could do terrible things to him or his family. Does he have a girlfriend? A fiancée? A wife? No, I don't think so. I hope not, anyway. I wonder what John and Sandra are thinking? Are they done? Have they given up? Am I on my own now?

Meanwhile, Ricardo walked a familiar ocean-side trail near his family home, his thoughts as turbulent as the waves.

Escobar didn't have to let me go. Family connections are one thing, but those packs of gold are enormous. He could have just made my body disappear out there somewhere. Maybe he's afraid the Americans would turn him in. Lauren is so beautiful. And brave. She came down that mountain like a lioness. We barely know each other. Would she stay here on the island if we had the gold? What if we don't get it back? Can I live in America? Where does she even live? No idea. Will she want to go after that gold? Or will she want to back away, too afraid of Escobar to risk it? I want to go for it. We're young. It would change our lives. Lives spent together, or lives that will be separate? Now, I at least know where Escobar is. I'll bet I can get to his compound by boat. Then what? Lauren will have some ideas. We'll work it out tomorrow.

As exhaustion finally claimed them, their sleep was deep but restless. Dreams wove together their fears and hopes — nightmarish scenarios of capture and loss intermingled with visions of victory and romance. By morning, the raw edges of their trauma had softened, replaced by a steely determination. In the crucible of their shared ordeal, courage was forged, and plans took shape. The adventure, it seemed, would continue.

CHAPTER 27

GOOD PADDLING

"Can we please take a day off from dangerous treasure hunting?" Sandra pleaded. "My nerves are still doing the cha-cha from yesterday. I get that you're not ready to quit, but maybe we could just brainstorm today? You know, plot and scheme from the safety of a lounge chair?"

Lauren, sprawled by the outdoor pool with Sandra and John, awaited the assembly of their running group for the day's activity. She glanced at John, silently nominating him as the first responder to his wife's request.

John inhaled deeply, as if trying to suck in some courage along with the salty air. "All right, dear. I suppose we do need a better plan if we're going to take on the local mobster. I just wish we could sic the police on him without ending up sleeping with the fishes ourselves." He turned to Lauren, his eyes pleading for backup.

"I'm cool with whatever you decide." Lauren shrugged, her nonchalance masking the rapid-fire text conversation she'd been having with Ricardo all morning. Their covert planning session was brewing up a scheme that might just work with no one ending up dead. No need to spill those beans to the Crismans just yet, though. She fired off another quick text: "Crismans need a breather. It's you and me today, partner in crime."

"Thank you." Sandra sighed with relief. "Now, when's our bus arriving?"

"Thirty minutes," John replied after checking his watch.

Suddenly, a caffeinated whirlwind swept onto the pool deck. "Who's ready to paddle their way to adventure?" Sheryl chirped. "Bus in thirty, folks! We missed you yesterday, so today, you get VIP seats at the front of the whale bus!"

Lauren opened her mouth to plead exhaustion from yesterday's escapades, but Sandra perked up unexpectedly. "Kayaking? Oh, we adore kayaking, don't we, John?"

Her husband's eyebrows shot up like startled seagulls. "Do we? I seem to recall it always ending in a fight."

"Oh, do tell." Sheryl leaned in, scenting juicy gossip.

Sandra rolled her eyes. "We don't fight. I just have to…guide him on the finer points of the correct stroke technique. He struggles to match my rhythm."

Sheryl and Lauren erupted into giggles. "Oh, honey," Sheryl replied, "I know exactly what you mean. My husband has the same issue. I swear, he's just splashing away in his own little world."

Sandra's face turned the shade of a ripe tomato. "No, no! I meant the paddling!"

Lauren, unable to resist, chimed in next. "A good paddler is worth their weight in gold. But finding one? That's the real treasure hunt."

John, deciding to join the fray, added, "And here I thought I was the Michael Phelps of paddling. Turns out, I might need some private lessons."

"Oh, stop it, all of you!" Sandra buried her face in her hands, peeking through her fingers like a blushing teenager.

Sheryl, still chuckling, steered the conversation back on course. "Alright, aquanauts, bus in fifteen!" She vanished inside, leaving a wake of laughter behind her.

Lauren stood, stretching languidly. "Well, I'd better go find myself a paddling partner. Maybe someone who knows how to handle their oar." With a wink, she sauntered off, leaving John and Sandra to contemplate the day's aquatic adventures—and perhaps a few paddling lessons.

CHAPTER 28

KAYAKING

The azure waters of the Atlantic lapped gently against the flotilla of brightly colored kayaks as the guide's voice carried across the waves. "We'll be hugging the coastline, folks. Keep at least a hundred meters from those rocky outcrops. No need to test your kayaking skills against Mother Nature just yet." His tanned hand swept along the horizon, drawing their attention to a series of dark openings in the distant cliffs. "See those caves carved into the rock face? That's our destination. If Neptune's in a good mood, we might even paddle through one. It's a natural tunnel that curves and spits you out the other side. I'll make the call when we get there."

"This is absolutely thrilling! Cave kayaking, what could be better?" Stacy's enthusiasm bubbled over, and she seemed to be almost vibrating in her excitement.

Lauren had not needed to find a partner, after all. Arriving at the bus, she'd felt a familiar touch on her arm and turned to see Stacy's eager face. "You're a kayaking pro, right? I'm a total newbie and could use an experienced partner." Lauren, recalling their last encounter at the whaling museum and the suspiciously snapped photo, hesitated briefly before acquiescing. "Sure, why not? I'll show you the ropes."

Now, as their little armada sliced through the waves, Lauren could hear Sandra's voice drifting from behind them, patiently explaining the finer points of paddle synchronization to John. Lauren turned to her own partner. "You're doing great, Stacy. Just keep a steady rhythm, and I'll match you."

Stacy, her hair whipping in the salty breeze, twisted around to face Lauren. "Where were you guys yesterday? We had a blast, and you were MIA."

"Hiking," Lauren replied, her tone carefully neutral. "We hired a guide to hike the volcano."

"Seriously? Aren't all these runs tough enough?"

Lauren's response was terse. "When you see a mountain, you climb it."

The kayaks converged around their guide, forming a loose circle near the imposing black lava cliffs. He gestured towards the last cave in the series, a gaping maw in the rock face. "This one's our ticket through to the other side. The ocean's relatively calm today, so it'll be a smooth ride…mostly."

Stacy's eyes widened as she stared into the inky darkness. "Smooth? That looks terrifying!"

Lauren's competitive spirit flared. "Oh, we're definitely going in. We didn't paddle all this way to chicken out now. Look around, nobody here's a pro. We're all in the same boat, literally."

The guide's last instructions echoed across the water. "Follow my lead if you're up for the cave. If not, hang back and enjoy the marine life." With that, he shot forward, perfectly aligned with the cave's center. The others fell into a ragged line behind him.

As they entered the cavern, the sounds of off-key singing floated back to them. "Yo ho, heave ho! A pirate's life for me!" Soon, the entire group had joined in, some belting out every word, others content with just the chorus.

The sunlight faded as they ventured deeper, and the water's surface became eerily still. Then, rounding a bend, they caught sight of daylight streaming through the exit.

Suddenly, Stacy leaned precariously over the side, pointing excitedly. "Look! A sea turtle!" She fumbled with the phone dangling from a lanyard around her neck, twisting to capture the creature's path.

In a heartbeat, Stacy's excitement turned to panic. With a yelp and a splash, she toppled into the water, her head bobbing up almost immediately thanks to her life jacket. "Help!" she sputtered, while her arms flailed around.

"You're okay," Lauren reassured her before extending an oar for her to grab onto. "Just breathe. Don't try to climb back in yet."

The guide materialized beside them, quickly assessing the situation and talking Stacy through the proper technique for re-entering a kayak from open water. Soon, the drenched but unharmed woman was back in her seat, and the group was receiving instructions for a safer return route.

As they paddled back, Lauren's mind raced. She remembered her own unexpected dip from a few days ago and John's suspicions about Stacy's guilty expression. "Well, now we're both members of the impromptu swimming club," Lauren quipped. "Though my plunge was a bit more...intense."

"It was terrifying," Stacy admitted, her voice still shaky. "The ocean's just so vast and unpredictable."

"Tell me about it. I got a firsthand lesson in that department."

Using the cover of her position at the rear of the kayak, Lauren deftly accessed the phone she'd swiped from Stacy

during the chaos of the rescue. The photo gallery confirmed her suspicions: shots of herself, the Crismans, and even Ricardo from their first meeting. The messaging app revealed a single contact labeled "V," with the incriminating photos attached.

Lauren tucked the phone away, her gaze boring into the back of Stacy's head. The pieces of the puzzle were falling into place. "Victor, you conniving bastard," she muttered under her breath, her mind already planning their next move in this game of cat and mouse.

ONE STEP CLOSER

"Where's my phone?" Stacy's panicked voice cut through the post-kayaking chatter as she clambered out of the boat onto the dock.

Lauren, feigning nonchalance, pointed to the kayak's floor. "It's right there." Without waiting for a response, she turned and walked away, her mind already racing with the information she'd gleaned.

Once alone, Lauren fired off a detailed text to Ricardo, recounting the kayaking adventure and her discoveries from Stacy's phone. They agreed that Ricardo should keep a low profile by avoiding any visible contact with Lauren or the Crismans for the rest of their stay. However, invisibility didn't preclude proximity. Ricardo sent her the address of a discreet restaurant within walking distance of the hotel, arranging a clandestine lunch meeting.

The restaurant was a hidden gem, its rustic charm amplified by the aroma of grilled fish and the gentle clinking of glasses. Lauren and Ricardo sat across from each other, their eyes meeting over plates of succulent fish, fragrant rice, and colorful vegetables.

"I'm certain the mysterious 'V' in her contacts is Victor," Lauren said in a low voice. "But I can't figure out how he roped her into this espionage game. So far, she's just been my shadow."

Ricardo nodded with a serious expression. "And reporting every move you make back to Escobar."

"Exactly," Lauren agreed. "So, what's our next play?"

Ricardo leaned in, his voice dropping to a conspiratorial whisper. "Susana gave me a lead on Escobar's residence here on the island. I've scouted it from the sea. There's a private dock, making access relatively straightforward."

"Guards?" Lauren asked.

Ricardo chuckled, the sound warming Lauren's heart. "That's Hollywood talking. Here, his reputation is all the security he needs."

"And you think that's where he's stashed the gold?"

"It makes the most sense. He wouldn't risk keeping it at any of his businesses where his employees might stumble upon it."

Ricardo then outlined his plan in meticulous detail. Lauren listened intently, asking pointed questions about her role. After a thorough discussion, she nodded her agreement.

Lauren sighed after glancing at her watch. "I should head back. Global Runners has an evening run through the old vineyards, ending with a wine tasting and dinner. I was planning on a quick poolside nap to recharge after kayaking."

"And all this exercise passes for a vacation in your world?" Ricardo teased.

"Of course! We can't miss a thing if this is our only visit to the islands." The moment the words left her mouth, Lauren felt a pang in her chest. She hadn't considered the finality of her time with Ricardo. Her plan had always been to return to America, to her version of normal life. Looking into Ricardo's eyes, she saw her own sadness mirrored there. "Well," she added softly, "I could always come back."

Hope flickered across Ricardo's face as he reached for her hand. "Or," he said, his voice barely above a whisper, "you could stay."

Lauren's breath caught in her throat. She tilted her head, echoing, "Stay?" The possibility she'd never entertained before now suddenly seemed alluring.

Outside the restaurant, Lauren wrapped her arms around Ricardo, tilting her head back to meet his gaze. He leaned down to capture her lips in a kiss that left them both breathless. When they finally parted, Lauren murmured, "I really should go."

Ricardo's eyes sparkled with mischief. "Or you could come with me. Perhaps that nap isn't as essential as you thought."

A slow, sultry smile spread across Lauren's face. "You know, I'm suddenly feeling very rested."

Hand in hand, they strolled away from the restaurant, their steps light and purposeful. As they rounded a corner, Ricardo pulled Lauren close, whispering something in her ear that made her laugh. She playfully swatted his arm before leaning into him, their bodies moving in perfect sync.

The afternoon sun cast long shadows as they approached Ricardo's house, a charming, little villa nestled among fragrant citrus trees. Lauren paused at the threshold, her eyes meeting Ricardo's with a mix of excitement and anticipation. He opened the door with a flourish, gesturing for her to enter.

"Welcome to my humble abode."

Lauren stepped inside, and her gaze roamed appreciatively over the sun-drenched interior. She turned to face Ricardo, her expression a blend of desire and playfulness. "So, about that nap."

Ricardo closed the door behind them, the soft click echoing with promise. "I have a feeling," he murmured, drawing her close, "that sleep is the last thing on either of our minds right now."

As the afternoon light filtered through the windows, casting a golden glow over the room, Lauren and Ricardo lost themselves in each other, the world outside fading away into insignificance.

WINE COUNTRY

The hotel's glass doors swung open, admitting Lauren along with a gust of salty air. Sandra, lounging in the lobby, raised an eyebrow. "Where have you been? I thought we were going to catch some rays by the pool."

Lauren's cheeks flushed, and not just from the afternoon heat. "Oh, I explored the town, grabbed lunch at this quaint local place." She aimed for nonchalance, but her eyes sparkled with barely contained excitement.

Sandra glanced at her watch, skepticism etched on her face. "Hmm. Must have been quite the lunch."

"It was…delicious," Lauren replied, a secret smile playing on her lips. "I might go back tomorrow."

Changing the subject, Sandra asked, "The vineyard run starts soon. Will you be ready?"

"Just need to freshen up. Back in a flash!" Lauren dashed to her room, but her mind still lingered on her encounter with Ricardo.

An hour later, the Global Runners gathered in the hotel's courtyard, a sea of colorful athletic wear against the backdrop of black lava walls. Madelena's charm seeped into the very air—a blend of ocean breeze, sunbaked stone, and the faint scent of grapes.

Sheryl, their effervescent leader, addressed the group. "Everyone feeling the burn? Kayaking this morning, four days of running—now that's a vacation!" She passed the mic to Gina, her ever-reliable second-in-command.

Gina led them through stretches, her voice steady and reassuring. "The course is clearly marked. You'll weave through town, then into one of the island's largest vineyards. Watch your footing on the lava rocks and feel free to pause for photos. There's a surprise in the last mile—I won't spoil it, but stay alert."

With a rallying cry of "Global Runners…Go!" the group surged forward. Their collective energy felt palpable.

Lauren fell into step with John and Sandra, choosing companionship over speed. The cobblestone streets of

Madelena gave way to narrower paths, the transition from town to vineyard as seamless as brushstrokes on a canvas.

When they were out of earshot of the others, Lauren murmured, "I know where Escobar is living. He's in Baixa."

John's eyebrows shot up. "How did you come by that information?"

"Susana knows everything on this island," Lauren replied, omitting Ricardo's involvement to protect him.

"And what? We just knock on his door and ask for the gold back?" John's tone was skeptical.

"No, but maybe we could alert the antiquities authorities to search his house," Lauren suggested.

John nodded thoughtfully. "Possibly, if we had proof that he's holding something of historical significance."

Their conversation trailed off as they entered the vineyard grounds. The landscape before them was a testament to human perseverance—a sea of basalt lava transformed into thriving grape vines. Everywhere they looked, small holes had been painstakingly chipped into the volcanic rock and filled with imported soil from Faial Island. The sheer scope of the endeavor was staggering.

Three-foot lava rock walls crisscrossed the terrain, creating a labyrinth of protection for the vines. These walls shielded the plants from the wind and salt spray while trapping the sun's warmth, creating a microclimate perfect for viticulture. Lauren marveled at the ingenuity, feeling as though she'd stepped onto an alien world.

The gravel road ended abruptly, giving way to a narrow path squeezed between two lava walls. Barely two feet wide, it was a challenging route, even for a single person. Loose rocks littered the ground, having tumbled from the walls over decades. The treacherous footing reminded Lauren of the lava tube where she'd discovered the chest of gold coins.

Her hand instinctively moved to her pocket, fingers brushing against the single coin she carried. The cool metal against her skin triggered a flood of memories— finding the treasure, the thrill of discovery, and most prominently, her relationship with Ricardo. Their most recent rendezvous replayed in her mind, sending a shiver down her spine, despite the afternoon heat.

As she carefully navigated the rocky path, Lauren's thoughts swirled like a tempest. *Stay on the island? Return home? Pursue the gold? Let it go?* And at the center of it all—Ricardo. His warm eyes, his strong hands, the way he made her feel alive in a way she hadn't in years.

The path wound on, mirroring the twists and turns of Lauren's internal struggle. With each step, she felt herself moving closer to a crossroads, knowing that soon she'd have to make a choice that would alter the course of her life forever.

CHARCUTERIE AND CONFRONTATION

The vineyard path abruptly gave way to the island's unique shoreline, catching Lauren off-guard. Before her stretched a fifty-foot-wide strip of beach, but calling it a beach would be a gross exaggeration. It was a treacherous field of massive lava boulders, each one a formidable obstacle.

Lauren's pace slowed dramatically as she adapted to this strange terrain. She took three quick steps across the first boulder, then leaped across a crevice to land precariously on the next. The race markers protruded from gaps between rocks, stretching into the distance like a gauntlet.

Her muscles burned with each leap, her heart pounding not just from exertion, but from the constant risk of a misstep. One wrong move could mean a twisted ankle, or worse. The roar of the nearby ocean seemed to mock her efforts.

Finally, mercifully, Lauren spotted the finish line. As she crossed, the cheers of her fellow runners washed over her like a wave of relief. "I didn't know if I was a runner or an astronaut out there," she said in between taking deep breaths and high-fiving the others.

The group, buzzing with adrenaline and shared stories of their boulder-hopping ordeal, followed Sheryl towards their next destination. The winery loomed before them, its white, fortress-like walls a striking contrast to the rugged landscape they'd just conquered.

As they entered the long, shadowy corridor of the winery, servers offered them all glasses of wine. Before them stretched an enormous table, disappearing into the darkness like some fantastical illusion. "That's the longest charcuterie board in the world!" Sandra exclaimed.

The runners, famished from their ordeal, eagerly filled their plates. John and Sandra searched for a quiet corner with their plates and glasses clutched tightly in their hands. Suddenly, John froze, his face draining of color. Sandra followed his gaze to a familiar, unwelcome figure approaching them with a predatory grin.

"Good evening, treasure hunters." Duarte Escobar's voice was as smooth as silk, but with an underlying edge that set their nerves on fire. "Welcome to my winery." His gesture encompassed the entire facility, a subtle reminder of his power and reach.

John and Sandra stood rigidly, and their shock was palpable. Escobar's lips curled into a cold smile. "There's no need for concern. I have what I want. You aren't a threat to me." His words, meant to reassure the married couple, only heightened the tension. His eyes scanned the crowd. "I see your partner, that impetuous young woman, back there. But I don't see the young man."

John, seizing the chance to protect Ricardo, quickly replied, "He was just a hired guide, not a partner. We don't need him anymore. He made it clear he's afraid to cross you."

"He is wise," Escobar purred before reaching into his pocket. The movement made John and Sandra flinch involuntarily. "I've brought you a souvenir. A small thank you for all your…work."

Three small coins dropped into John's palm. In the dim light, their golden sheen seemed to mock him, a reminder of all they had lost. John's emotions warred within him—anger, frustration, fear, and a burning desire for revenge. With great effort, he managed a neutral response. "Thank you. We hunt treasure for the adventure. One coin is as good as one hundred to us."

Escobar's laugh was like ice water down their spines. "Foolish, but a healthy attitude, given the situation."

Sandra remained silent, her jaw clenched, her eyes never leaving Escobar's face. Her silence spoke volumes about her barely contained fury.

Across the room, Lauren watched the exchange with a growing alarm. Her mind raced, torn between fear for her friends' safety and an overwhelming desire for retribution.

Unnoticed by all, Stacy observed from a shadowy corner, methodically chewing on a piece of sausage. Her eyes darted between the group and Escobar, absorbing every detail of the tense confrontation.

The air in the winery seemed to thicken, the chatter of the other runners fading to a distant hum. In this moment, it was just Sandra, John, Lauren, and Escobar, locked in a silent battle of wills, with the weight of stolen treasure and unspoken threats hanging between them.

PYRRHIC RECOVERY

Lauren's fingers trembled as she typed the message to Ricardo: "Escobar at winery. Now is your chance. Be careful." She glanced over her shoulder, half-expecting to see Escobar's menacing figure looming behind her. The night air felt thick with danger and possibility.

They hadn't told the Crismans about the plan to search Escobar's home. It was clearly risky and perhaps more dangerous than the older couple would have agreed to, but Lauren and Ricardo were certain the gold had to be there.

Under the cover of darkness, Ricardo guided his small boat to the dock behind Escobar's home. The gentle lapping of waves against the hull seemed deafening in the stillness. He held his breath, straining to detect any sign of life from the house. The rustle of pine needles, the distant cry of a night bird, the rhythmic crash of waves on the shore—all normal sounds that still set his nerves on edge.

Satisfied he was alone, Ricardo crept up the rocky slope, wincing at every pebble that shifted under his feet. The unlocked back door seemed both a blessing and a trap. He slipped inside, his eyes adjusting to the dimness of the opulent sitting room. Couches, chairs, tables, and a bar suggested this space was primarily used for entertaining.

Too many people, Ricardo decided. *Not a good place to hide two bags of gold.* He pressed on and continued his search.

Room by room, Ricardo looked everywhere, his heart pounding so loudly that he feared it might give him away. Finally, he reached an office—a physical representation of Escobar's power and influence. Standing at the door, Ricardo surveyed the interior. Large mahogany desk. A case of books and papers. A ledge populated with framed pictures, small trophies, and a strange assortment of trinkets. Leaning against one wall, Ricardo recognized the large curving rib bone of a whale. Hanging from the ceiling by invisible lines, the skull of another small whale. Both items were difficult to come by now. Ricardo guessed that, like other residents of the islands, Escobar had inherited these skeletal remains from his father or grandfather. The presence of these valuable heirlooms encouraged him to think that this house was the perfect place to store a treasure.

Ricardo's methodical search led him to the closet. His breath caught as he spotted two familiar shapes. Reaching out with shaking hands, he felt the telltale clink of coins. Elation surged through him as he snapped a photo and sent it with a triumphant "Jackpot!" to Lauren.

As silently as possible, he lifted the larger of the two bags. He remembered the familiar weight from the hike down the side of the volcano, but that was when he realized he couldn't carry both bags out of here. Ricardo's stomach twisted as he realized he'd have to leave one behind.

Hoisting the pack up onto his shoulders, he slung the straps into place and went back the way he came out of the house. Every step towards freedom felt like an eternity, the bag growing heavier with each passing moment. He reached the backdoor and was slipping through it when he heard the click and squeak of another door opening.

Just as escape seemed within reach, a voice shattered the silence. "Hello? *Senhor* Escobar?"

Ricardo's blood turned to ice. Victor. Lauren's ex. Escobar's muscle.

With agonizing slowness, Ricardo eased the door shut and began his treacherous descent. The bag, once a prize, now felt like a death sentence. He stumbled, and the sound of shifting rocks felt impossibly loud in the quiet night.

A rectangle of light spilled from the opened door. "Hello? Who's out there?" Victor's silhouette loomed on the porch as he scanned the darkness.

Ricardo pressed himself against a tree, hardly daring to breathe. His lungs burned, and sweat trickled down his back. He willed himself to become one with the shadows, praying to any god who would listen.

Victor didn't leave and instead stayed on the porch, listening intently for any sounds that didn't belong. Ricardo was as still as a statue. Minutes that felt like hours passed. Finally, the other man returned inside the house, closing the door behind him.

Ricardo used the reprieve to rush to the bottom of the slope. *Has Victor given up, or will he return with a flashlight?* Ricardo couldn't afford to find out. Arriving at his waiting boat, he shrugged off the pack and struggled to place it quietly inside. As he did so, he fell from the dock into the boat. The pack hit the edge and spilled a few gold coins onto the deck. However, the considerable weight of the bag caused it to topple over the edge, and it sank immediately beneath the waves. Ricardo's eyes were wide with dread. Their treasure was gone.

Horror and disbelief paralyzed him. Their careful planning, the risks they'd taken, all for nothing. The treasure was beyond his reach, meters beneath the sea.

At that moment, a beam of light cut through the darkness, spurring Ricardo into action. He lunged for the coins laying on the dock and pushed off from the dock, lying flat in the boat as the current carried him away. Each second stretched into an agonizing eternity as he waited for the shout of discovery, the crack of gunfire.

As the distance grew between him and Escobar's property, the magnitude of his failure settled over him like a suffocating blanket. *How can I face Lauren? How can I explain that our dreams have slipped through my fingers?*

The gentle rocking of the boat felt like a mockery of comfort. Ricardo stared up at the star-filled sky, the same sky that had witnessed their initial discovery on the mountain. It seemed to laugh at him, a cruel joke from the universe.

He knew a simple text wouldn't suffice. He'd have to look Lauren in the eyes and confess how close they'd come, only to lose everything in a moment of clumsiness. The weight of that impending conversation pressed down on him, far heavier than the bag of gold had ever been.

As the boat drifted further from shore, Ricardo closed his eyes, trying to steel himself for the crushing disappointment he was about to deliver. The taste of near victory had turned bitter in his mouth, leaving only the ashes of what might have been.

DEADLY RECKONING

Duarte Escobar strode into his home, intoxicated by his own perceived brilliance. The satisfaction of intimidating the Crismans lingered on his tongue like a fine wine. His triumph eclipsed all his previous conquests, including the restaurants he snatched and the ports he manipulated. He was unstoppable.

The unexpected glow of lights pierced his euphoria. "Victor?" he barked, irritation creeping into his voice.

His hired muscle lounged on the couch with his eyes glued to his phone. He was smiling as he tapped out a text. "Thought I heard something earlier," Victor mumbled, and he didn't even bother to look up. "Probably just the wind."

Escobar's lip curled in disgust. *This laid back, lazy attitude of his was the difference between greatness and mediocrity—how a person used their time greatly affected the outcome of their future.* He turned away from Victor in curt silence.

Inside his massive bedroom, Escobar kicked off his shoes and collapsed onto the opulent bed. Images of intimidating John Crisman floated through his mind. These transformed into crisp pictures of gold coins. He imagined them in a jewel encrusted chest sitting in his living room. Then, he painted an image of a party filled with his friends, business partners, and there were even a few government officials. Holding expensive drinks, they loitered around the glittering mountain of wealth, envious of him, wishing they could be him.

The imaginary picture excited him. It awoke a lust in his heart, a hunger to feel the golden bounty slipping through his fingers. He rose and made his way to the office. The office closet yawned open, and Escobar's world imploded. Where two bags should have rested, only one remained. His mind reeled, unable to process the loss. Then, like a volcano erupting, rage consumed him.

He snatched his pistol and stalked back into the living room. His eyes, now feral with fury, locked onto Victor. "You miserable thief!" he snarled as he raised the gun.

Victor's head snapped up, his confusion morphing into terror as he registered the weapon. Escobar was too caught up in his anger to register the phone in Victor's hands. "Boss? What?"

"Don't play dumb!" Escobar roared, and spittle flew from his lips. "Half my gold, gone! And here you sit, the only one in the house!"

Victor scrambled to his feet, dropping his phone in his rush to do so, with his hands raised and eyes wild with panic. "No! I swear, I haven't touched it!" His voice cracked, desperation clear in every syllable.

Escobar's finger tightened on the trigger. His face was a mask of murderous rage. "You thought you could outsmart me? That I wouldn't notice?"

"Please," Victor begged, his legs trembling beneath him. "It must've been an intruder. Remember the noise I mentioned earlier? Someone broke in!"

"Liar!" Escobar bellowed before advancing further into the room and closer to Victor. "Nothing's broken. Just my trust in you, you worthless piece of shit!"

Victor's mind raced, grasping for any lifeline he could find. "Lauren! The old couple! They know about the gold. It had to be them!"

Escobar's laugh was bitter, devoid of humor. "You take me for a fool? They were with me, cowering like the weaklings they are. But you—you were here, alone with my gold."

"No, please," Victor whimpered. Tears welled in his eyes. He could taste his own fear, acrid and overwhelming. "I'm telling the truth. I wouldn't betray you!"

For a moment, the only sound was Victor's ragged breathing and the thunderous pounding of his heart. Victor never heard the sound of the gun. The bullet entered his heart before the sound reached his ears. He didn't gasp in astonishment. He didn't regret the end of his life. In an instant, Victor simply ceased to be alive. His body dropped to the polished wooden floor, blood seeping from a single hole in his chest. His phone laid at his side, the only witness to his last moments.

As the echo of the shot faded, so, too, did Escobar's blind rage. Cold calculation returned to his eyes as he surveyed the scene. This situation was a mess, but not an unfamiliar one. His fingers flew across his phone: "Cleanup. My house. Now."

Escobar turned away from the corpse, his mind already racing ahead. Victor had no friends on the island. He had few places to go. The missing bag of gold was nearby, and he would find it. No one stole from Duarte Escobar and lived to tell the tale. No one.

LOVE'S BITTER COIN

The winery's grand wooden doors creaked shut, signaling the end of a tense evening. Lauren lingered in the shadows, her heart racing with anticipation and fear. "Sandra," she whispered and beckoned the older woman closer.

John and Sandra approached. Their faces were etched with a mixture of relief and dejection. "That was… something," John muttered, his voice heavy with conflicting emotions.

Lauren's eyes darted around, ensuring their privacy. "What happened in there?"

John recounted their encounter with Escobar, his words painting a vivid picture of the couple's powerlessness. With each detail, Lauren felt a knot tightening in her stomach, and her thoughts constantly drifted to Ricardo and their audacious plan.

"It's both crushing and oddly comforting," John concluded as he produced three gleaming coins from his pocket. "Escobar's little 'souvenir' for us. A trophy of his victory, I suppose."

As the cool metal touched her palm, Lauren's fingers instinctively curled around it. The weight of the coin felt insignificant compared to the bounty she expected from Ricardo. Guilt gnawed at her as she bid the Crismans goodnight, their innocence in opposition to her complicity.

Hours ticked by, each moment stretching Lauren's nerves to their breaking point. When Ricardo's cryptic message finally arrived, relief flooded through her veins. She rushed to their meeting point, her mind spinning with visions of gold and a future intertwined with Ricardo's.

The headlights of Ricardo's van cut through the darkness, and Lauren's heart soared. She flung herself into the vehicle, her arms wrapping around Ricardo's neck. "I was so worried," she breathed, leaning in for a kiss, but something was off. Ricardo's response was tepid, and his embrace lacked its usual warmth.

As they drove to a secluded spot, Lauren's excitement morphed into unease. She strained to see the backpacks in the darkness, her imagination filling the void with gleaming treasures. When they finally stopped, Ricardo's face in the dim light told her everything she needed to know before he uttered a word.

Ricardo's tale unfolded like a nightmare. The initial triumph of infiltrating Escobar's home gave way to a harrowing escape and a devastating loss. With each word, Lauren felt her dreams crumbling, replaced by a cold, harsh reality.

"These…these are all that's left," Ricardo said, his voice barely above a whisper as he offered her a coffee cup containing a pitiful handful of coins.

Lauren stared at the meager offering, her mind reeling. The weight of those few coins felt like a mockery of the fortune they'd nearly grasped. She wanted to comfort Ricardo, to assure him that his safety was what truly mattered, but the words stuck in her throat. She was choked by disappointment and a growing sense of shame.

As silence engulfed them, Lauren felt something shift within her. The warmth she'd felt for Ricardo cooled, replaced by a gnawing emptiness. She recoiled from this feeling, horrified at the realization that their bond might have been forged more by gold than genuine affection.

"You should take most of these," Ricardo finally said, with downcast eyes. "Share them with the Crismans. It's easier to explain a few coins, anyway."

Lauren shook her head, unable to bear the thought of those coins as a constant reminder of what they'd lost—both in treasure and in each other. "No, you keep them. You risked everything to get them back." Her voice sounded hollow, even to her own ears.

She leaned in, planting a chaste kiss on Ricardo's cheek. It felt like a goodbye. "I need to think," she murmured and slipped out of the van and into the night before he could protest.

As Lauren walked away, each step felt heavier than the last. The cool night air did nothing to clear her tumultuous thoughts. She'd entered this adventure seeking treasure and excitement, possibly even love. Now, she questioned everything—her motivations, her feelings, her very character.

Back in the van, Ricardo sat motionless, the small cup of coins mocking him. A solitary tear traced its way down his cheek, carrying with it the weight of lost dreams and a love that had barely begun to bloom before withering on the vine.

The night enveloped them both, two souls now adrift, separated by the very thing that had brought them together. The promise of gold had ignited their passion, and its loss now threatened to extinguish the fragile flame of their budding romance.

CHAPTER 35

ELIMINATION

The acrid smell of industrial-strength cleaning agents permeated the air as Escobar's henchman meticulously scrubbed away the last traces of Victor's existence from the living room floor. The cleaner, a burly man with calloused hands and dead eyes, moved with practiced efficiency, erasing blood spatter and scuff marks with equal indifference.

In the adjacent office, Duarte Escobar sat behind his mahogany desk, his fingers tracing the contours of a single gold coin. The weight of it, both physical and metaphorical, consumed his thoughts as he turned it over and over in his hands. Crown side to *figa* side, a rhythmic motion that matched the ticking of his mind.

"One coin," he mused, his voice barely above a whisper, "melted down is $2,000." He studied the simple design. "But as an artifact of Sebastian's rule? Priceless."

His gaze shifted to the closet where the remaining bag of gold sat. The mental calculations came easily to him, as he was a man accustomed to weighing value against risk. "Sixty pounds of gold melted down is two million dollars. 1,000 Sebastian coins, priceless times a thousand." A mirthless chuckle escaped his lips.

But the satisfaction was hollow, incomplete. The shadow of what was lost loomed large in his mind. "But the bigger bag was a hundred pounds. Three million dollars can't just get away."

Escobar's eyes narrowed as he spread several coins across his desk, each one representing a player in this dangerous game. With deliberate movements, he pushed them forward, one by one.

"Victor, in my house." The first coin glinted under the office light.

"Old woman, at the winery." The second joined its companion.

"Old man, at the winery." The third coin clinked softly against the others.

"Young woman, Victor's girlfriend, at the winery." The fourth completed the line.

As he contemplated the arrangement, a knock on the office door interrupted his thoughts. "Come," he commanded in a flat and controlled tone.

The cleaner entered, his massive frame filling the doorway. His shaved head gleamed with sweat, and the gap where his front tooth should have been gave his otherwise menacing appearance an oddly vulnerable quality.

"*Senhor* Escobar, it's finished. All clean. I'll take care of…the pieces." The man's voice was gruff but respectful, aware of the delicate nature of his work.

Escobar rose from his chair, approaching the loyal servant with measured steps. Without a word, he pressed a thick fold of euro notes into the man's hand, their eyes meeting in a moment of unspoken understanding.

"For you, Carlos," Escobar said quietly. "And your family will be taken care of."

Gratitude flashed briefly across Carlos' stoic face. "Thank you, *Senhor* Escobar." With a nod, he disappeared as silently as he had arrived.

The moment the door closed, Escobar sprang into action. His mind raced with possibilities as he combed every corner of the house. Each room held the potential for revelation, but as he moved from space to space, his frustration mounted.

The garage yielded nothing, nor did the back porch. Undeterred, Escobar made his way down the slope behind the house, his eyes scanning the ground for any sign of disturbance. The moonlight cast long shadows across the rocky terrain, playing tricks on his vision, but he pressed on. At the water's edge, Escobar paused, his gaze sweeping across the gentle waves lapping at the shore.

But fate, it seemed, had not abandoned him entirely. A glint caught his eye, a flash of gold on the dark wooden dock.

Raising the coin to eye level, he scrutinized it, a humorless smile playing at the corners of his mouth. "So, you went this way, did you?" he murmured, addressing the inanimate object as if it could reveal its secrets.

The pieces of the puzzle fell into place in Escobar's mind. The coin's presence here, at the base of his property, spoke volumes. Someone had been here, someone who had seen the gold, someone who knew where to look.

"Who?" Escobar asked aloud, his voice barely audible above the gentle lapping of the waves. He stared at the coin for a long moment, his mind sifting through the possibilities, eliminating suspects one by one.

And then, like a bolt of lightning, clarity struck. "The guide," Escobar said, his eyes widening with realization. "My remote nephew."

The connection, once made, seemed obvious. The guide, Ricardo, had the means, the opportunity, and now Escobar realized the motive. The young man's apparent closeness to Victor's girlfriend, his knowledge of the island, his family connection, however distant, it all pointed to his involvement.

Escobar's jaw clenched, a mixture of anger and grudging admiration coursing through him. It was a bold move, one that spoke of desperation or remarkable courage—perhaps both.

As he pocketed the coin and turned back towards the house, Escobar's mind was already planning his next move. The guide may have won this round, but the game was far from over. Escobar had built his empire on cunning and ruthlessness, and he wasn't about to let an upstart nephew, no matter how resourceful, best him.

"You've played well, boy," Escobar muttered as he climbed the slope, his eyes glinting with determination. "But you've no idea who you're dealing with."

The night air carried his words away, a promise and a threat intertwined. As Escobar reached the house, his plan was clear. He knew where to go next, and this time, there would be no loose ends.

RICHES OR ROMANCE

The early morning sunlight cast long shadows across the hotel patio as Lauren spotted Sandra at the buffet. With a heavy heart, she motioned her friend to a secluded table, desperately seeking a moment of privacy.

Sandra's brow furrowed with concern as she sat down. "What's the matter, dear? You look terribly sad."

Lauren's eyes, rimmed with red from a sleepless night, met Sandra's. "It shows that badly?"

"I'm afraid it does," Sandra replied gently.

Taking a deep breath, Lauren steeled herself for the confession that had been eating away at her. "There's so much to tell you. I haven't been completely honest with you and John. I always meant well, but it turns out that I can't handle everything myself."

Sandra sipped her coffee, her expression open and patient. "Okay," she said simply, inviting Lauren to continue.

"You've probably noticed the relationship between Ricardo and me. We've become quite close…or we were, anyway," Lauren began in a wavering voice.

Sandra nodded, and a hint of a smile played on her lips. "Yes, it was pretty obvious. He's quite handsome, and he did help us out of that tight situation on the mountain."

Lauren's eyes misted over as she continued, "Well, we've been together a few times." She paused, making sure Sandra understood her meaning. "And he has always been wonderful. We were even considering a life together after this vacation. I mean, we didn't talk about details, but we were both wondering what came next."

"Were? But not anymore?" Sandra asked.

Lauren's composure cracked, and a tear escaped down her cheek. "I'll get to that. But it's all my fault." She took a moment to collect herself before diving into the full story of their ill-fated plan to recover the gold.

As Lauren recounted the events of the previous night, Sandra listened intently, her expression shifting from surprise to worry to understanding. When Lauren reached the part about the backpack of coins falling into the ocean, her voice broke with disappointment.

Sandra leaned in and placed a comforting hand on top of hers. "So, that's good news. Ricardo is safe. Escobar doesn't know it was him. We're no worse off than before. Plus, Escobar lost half of his stolen treasure. But I sense there's more you need to tell me."

Lauren's shoulders slumped. "I…I've been terrible. When I heard that the gold was gone, I felt the love in my heart melt away. I thought I was a good person. But when the future with Ricardo wasn't one of fabulous wealth, I wasn't sure I wanted to be with him anymore. I pushed him away last night, like he was nothing to me."

"I see," Sandra murmured. Her eyes filled with empathy.

"But he isn't nothing," Lauren insisted, her voice rising with emotion. "The shock of losing everything was just overwhelming. It shorted out all my other emotions. I've been so stupid, so…so shallow."

"You're not shallow, dear. You're human. You're just dealing with a lot. What do you want to do now?"

Tears flowed freely down Lauren's cheeks as she wrestled with her conflicting emotions. "My head tells me to leave the islands as fast as I can. Get out before Escobar comes looking for us. I could hop over to Lisbon today and feel safe."

"And your heart?" Sandra prodded gently.

Lauren's voice was barely above a whisper. "Find Ricardo. Tell him I'm sorry, that I made a mistake. Tell him I want to see where this goes. Stay with him in case something dangerous happens."

Sandra nodded, a knowing smile playing on her lips. "Well, that's all pretty clear. You just have to choose a course of action and then live with it."

"But what if he doesn't forgive me?" Lauren's voice cracked with vulnerability. "Maybe he just wants to go back to his simple, safe life as an adventure guide. Maybe I've ruined everything."

Sandra chuckled softly. "You don't know men, dear. He's waiting for you to get over your emotions. He's just waiting for you to let him know everything is alright."

Lauren looked up, hope and disbelief warring in her eyes. "How can you be so sure?"

"Because love, real love, isn't about gold or riches," Sandra said. Her voice was warm with wisdom. "It's about connection, about finding someone who sees the best in you, even when you can't see it yourself. And from what you've told me, Ricardo seems to be that kind of man."

Lauren's breath caught in her throat. "But I pushed him away. I let my greed overshadow everything else."

"And now you've realized your mistake," Sandra pointed out. "That's growth, Lauren. That's the self-awareness that makes relationships stronger."

"Do you really think he'd give me another chance?" Lauren asked.

Sandra's eyes twinkled as she glanced over Lauren's shoulder. "Why don't you ask him yourself?" From their table on the patio overlooking the hotel parking lot, Sandra pointed toward a familiar vehicle. "Isn't that his van parked down there?"

"Oh, my God!" Lauren blurted out as she leapt to her feet, her heart racing with renewed hope.

As Lauren rushed to the parking lot, Sandra called after her, "Treasure in your heart is better than treasure in your pocket, dear."

CHAPTER 37

FINAL RUN

Lauren's reunion with Ricardo had been tearful and passionate, their apologies accompanied by enthusiastic hugs and kisses in full view of the hotel. Sandra had witnessed the beginning of the scene before retreating inside, where she shared a nostalgic smile with John, reminiscing about their own former relationship trials.

"We did that?" John asked.

"Regularly," Sandra replied.

John turned back to his coffee and traditional Portuguese pasties, mumbling, "I don't think so."

"Who's ready for another run?" Sheryl's musical voice rang out, rousing the group. "Today is our last one. You'll want to have your swimming suit in your day bags. We finish at an ocean park."

As the bus departed for the starting line, Lauren and Ricardo, having completed their reconciliation, watched it leave before climbing into their own vehicle.

The starting line was set in a peaceful city park filled with grills, picnic tables, and playground equipment. Gina led the group in stretching exercises and briefed them on the course. "We'll descend from the park and follow a trail through the woods in that direction," she explained, pointing. "The terrain will change several times along the five-mile course. But you'll see markers. You can't get lost."

Just as Gina was about to send the group off, Lauren came bounding up to Sandra and John. "I'm going, too. I didn't want to miss the last group run."

"You're sure?" Sandra asked while glancing towards the parking area.

"He'll meet us at the finish line. He knows where it is," Lauren answered the unspoken question.

"Global Runners...Go!" Gina called, and the pack surged forward.

Tired from a lack of sleep, Lauren kept a steady pace with her treasure hunting compatriots. They descended into a beautiful wooded area lined with lush trees, enjoying the shade they provided. The earthy scent of moss and damp soil filled their lungs, invigorating their senses.

After long moments of silent running, John said, "We may not be rich, but we have memories of the adventure we shared and a single golden souvenir. I think that's a victory." Then, after a moment to think, he added, "With just one piece of gold, we won't have to bother with customs. It's just one more coin among the euro change in our pockets."

"Agreed," Lauren muttered. As an experienced treasure hunter, she knew the financial limits for crossing borders, but she also knew that declaring one ancient gold coin would lead to an interrogation by the authorities. It was a conversation she was eager to avoid.

They emerged from the trees to find themselves on top of a cliff overlooking the crashing ocean. The trail was a small path through a field of sharp lava rocks the size of marbles, magically devoid of troublesome debris.

"I'm guessing that centuries of locals and cattle walked this path to make it this clear," John observed.

The path undulated with the uneven top of the cliff, forcing them to climb up and then down small ridges only two feet high. Though the footing was clean and firm, it was by no means flat.

"Such a unique island. It's no wonder people compare these to Hawaii. Both archipelagos were formed by the same natural forces and left similar fingerprints on the land," Lauren mused.

Sandra added, "I've never run on terrain like this, and probably never will again." Then, after a moment of thought, she said, "I don't think this is the part I'll miss when we go home."

The mention of leaving the island pulled Lauren's mind back to an earlier question—whether to leave as scheduled or extend her stay. After this morning's reunion, she was certain she had the answer. The question no longer haunted her; it was now a pleasant thought.

The lava trail ended abruptly, and the group found themselves on a paved road through a small village. Soon, they were greeted by barking dogs. A pair of small terriers leaned precariously over the top of a wall, barking enthusiastically as each runner approached. They clearly considered the entire group to be trespassers on their territory.

John glanced up. "You look like a pair of killers," he taunted them.

Onward they ran, disturbing the peace of dogs all along the course, and the dogs disturbed the peace of their owners behind the walled homes.

Following a white painted wall with beautiful Spanish tiles along the top, Sandra suddenly stopped and pointed at the gates of someone's property. "Oh, look at that. The handles are pretty whales. One is a sperm whale, and the other is a blue whale. That's such a clever design."

Lauren's blood ran cold as she recognized the distinctive features Susana had described as markers of Escobar's home. Fear gripped her heart, and she encouraged her companions forward without explaining her sudden urgency.

As they exited the cluster of homes that made up the village, they found yet another small park nestled against the sea, and the fluttering flags that indicated the finish line. As usual, Sheryl and Gina were there with booming music, smiles, and high fives for everyone.

Lauren said, "We made it to the final finish." She was referring to both the racing vacation and the precarious adventure. The hard work was behind them. The rest was all a celebration.

"Time for a swim," John announced as he carried his suit to the waiting changing rooms.

Lauren turned her attention to the road, where she spotted the familiar van. She waved and ran to greet Ricardo, hoping he would join the group in the water.

As she jogged towards him, Lauren felt a mix of emotions. The exhilaration of completing the run, the lingering unease from seeing Escobar's house, and the joy of reuniting with Ricardo all swirled within her. The beauty of Pico Island surrounded them—the azure sea, the lush greenery, and the rugged volcanic landscape.

For a moment, Lauren allowed herself to bask in the warmth of the present. The camaraderie of her fellow runners, the sense of accomplishment, and the promise of Ricardo's company filled her with a tentative peace. She pushed aside the shadows of their recent ordeal, choosing instead to focus on the simple pleasures of the day.

As she reached Ricardo, their eyes met, and they shared a smile that spoke volumes. The journey had been perilous, but they had weathered it together. Now, with the sun shining down on the sparkling ocean before them, it appeared that they had finally reached a moment of true respite.

Little did they know that their hard-won peace was about to be shattered. Unseen eyes watched from the shadows, poised to drag them back into the heart of danger. But for now, in this fleeting instant, Lauren allowed herself to feel the simple joy of a run well-finished and the comfort of being with those she cared about most.

CHAPTER 38

ROADBLOCK

Lauren's body cut through the cool, churning ocean as she dove confidently from the concrete swimming platform. All around her, laughter and excited shouts filled the air as her fellow runners plunged into the refreshing water. Some wore swimsuits while others had impulsively jumped in still clad in their running gear. The joyous atmosphere was palpable—a fitting celebration to cap off an exhilarating and unforgettable week together.

As Lauren surfaced, she couldn't help but grin at the sight of her newfound friends splashing and playing in the water. They had traversed two islands from end to end, conquering dense forests, navigating rocky lava trails, scaling volcanic peaks, and braving the salty sea spray. After countless shared meals, drinks, and miles, they had become more than just fellow runners—they were family. This sense of closeness was the true magic of a Global Runners' event, the secret ingredient that made these trips so special.

From her sunny perch on the shore, Sheryl watched everyone with a warmth that radiated maternal pride. These vibrant individuals had become her extended family, their shared experiences forging bonds stronger than those she shared with some of her own relatives. The sight of their unbridled joy filled her heart with satisfaction.

Emerging from the surf, Lauren and Ricardo made their way to Sheryl, their skin glistening in the afternoon sun as they settled on either side of the race director.

"It's been a fantastic week." Lauren beamed, her eyes sparkling with genuine happiness.

Sheryl's face lit up at the remark. "I'm so glad to hear that! Does this mean we'll see you on future trips? There are so many new countries to explore."

Lauren leaned forward, catching Ricardo's eye with a playful glance. "I don't think I'm done exploring this one just yet."

"Oh, really?" Sheryl teased, and her eyebrows raised in amusement. "So, that's why you've been missing some of our group adventures. It was for this handsome fellow?"

Lauren's cheeks flushed slightly as she countered, "We had several of our own adventures."

Sheryl covered her ears. "TMI. You don't have to go into details."

Blushing, Lauren tried to recover. "No! That's not what I meant. It was the volcano, and…" She realized then that Sheryl's assumptions were exactly correct.

In an attempt to retreat from the embarrassment, Ricardo rose and announced, "I'm going to change into dry clothes."

When Lauren didn't move, Sheryl said with a mischievous smile, "Well? Aren't you going with him?"

"Umm…no?" Lauren paused only a second. "Well, actually, yes." Then, without another second of hesitation, she rose to follow Ricardo.

"Go get him, girl!" Sheryl shouted at her back.

Emerging from the changing rooms once she was done, Lauren took in the scene before her. The runners were still frolicking in the water, and their laughter carried on the sea breeze. A bittersweet feeling washed over her as she realized their time together was drawing to a close. They had only one evening left before they would part ways, scattering across the globe like seeds in the wind.

"Back to Madalena?" Ricardo asked while holding the van door open for her with a gentleman's flourish.

Lauren's eyes twinkled as she replied, "Sure, but let's stop by your place first. We need to get cleaned up." Her smile held a promise of more adventures to come, which was perfectly understood without any further explanation.

As they drove away from the ocean park, the sounds of merriment faded. Lauren's heart swelled with gratitude for the incredible experiences she'd shared with the Global Runners. The islands of the Azores had woven their magic, creating memories that would last a lifetime and opening doors to unexpected possibilities.

～ρ～ρ～ρ

The van wound its way along the narrow coastal road, the rhythmic hum of tires on asphalt suddenly interrupted by Ricardo's sharp intake of breath. Ahead, a hulking figure materialized in the middle of the road, his massive frame backlit by the sun. In one meaty fist, he clutched a length of pipe that glinted menacingly.

Ricardo's foot instinctively moved to the brake pedal, and the van slowed to a stop as his eyes darted left and right, seeking an escape route. But there was none to be found—high walls hemmed them in on both sides, leaving no room to maneuver.

Before Ricardo could shift into reverse, a heavy tap against the driver's side window made them both jump. Lauren's blood ran cold as she saw the unmistakable silhouette of a gun pressed against the glass, its muzzle a dark promise of violence. Behind it, the familiar features of Duarte Escobar came into focus. His eyes glittered with malice.

"Turn in there," Escobar commanded, gesturing with his weapon towards an open gate in the wall. Lauren's stomach dropped as she recognized the distinctive whale handles—they had unwittingly driven straight into the lion's den.

As they were herded out of the van and towards the house, the oppressive silence was broken only by the scrape of shoes on gravel and the labored breathing of Escobar's new muscle. This mountain of a man, with dead eyes and hands like sledgehammers, loomed behind them—a constant, wordless threat.

Inside, the tension in the air was palpable as Lauren finally found her voice. "What do you want with us? You have all the gold. You said we could go peacefully."

"I *had* all the gold," Escobar corrected. "But your boyfriend just couldn't leave it alone. He had to come looking for trouble."

"No! We didn't...he didn't..." was all she could manage. Then, needing to change the topic before her poor acting made the situation any worse, she inclined her head at the strange man who'd forced them to stop. She asked, "Where's Victor? I thought he was your muscle?"

Chuckling, Escobar said, "Victor was in the wrong place at the wrong time. At first, I was certain he'd betrayed me…just like he betrayed you. But then, I realized that he'd just failed to stop lover-boy here from slipping into the house. Sadly, by then, it was too late for Victor. Sorry about that."

The meaning of the words hit Lauren like a punch to the chest. She hated Victor for stealing everything from her, but she'd also loved him at one time. She carried so many wonderful memories of their years together. Losing him was like losing a piece of her past.

"You killed him?" Lauren stammered. She couldn't believe this situation could be real.

Escobar merely shrugged as if it was a necessary outcome.

"You bastard! For a worthless sack of gold?"

Escobar interrupted her tirade. "I'm glad you think it's worthless because I want it back. And you two are going to give it to me." He motioned for the other man to intervene.

The large man with the dead eyes clamped a hand on Ricardo's shoulder. It was like a vice closing on soft muscle. Ricardo yelped at the pain.

Lauren shouted, "We don't have it!"

"Obviously. But you know where it is. If you want to leave here alive, you'll tell me." Motioning to the thug, he explained, "He can do a lot to a man before he dies. It's not pretty to watch."

In agony, Ricardo muttered, "Tell him, Lauren."

"The gold is still here," she said. "I'll show you. Just let him go."

Escobar nodded at the thug, and his grip eased. "Okay, then show me. Quickly!"

Lauren and Ricardo led their captors to the back of the property and down to the water's edge. Ricardo moved to the spot where the boat had been docked. He pointed into the water. "Here. The bag fell out of the boat and sank. It was dark, and Victor was looking for me. So, I had to leave it."

Turning to his thug, Escobar said, "Get it."

The large man spoke for the first time. His voice was deep, but it was tinged with a little fear. "Is it deep? I don't swim."

"Well, find out. Get in there!"

The big man wadded into the water. It took just two steps before the water was up to his waist. Then, he bent forward, probing for the bottom with his fingers. As he reached left and right, his face skimmed the top of the water. He took an enormous breath and fully immersed himself in the water.

Everything was silent for a long moment. Then, there was a splashing as the man's big head emerged. He gasped and sputtered for air. Standing upright, he lifted the sodden backpack from the water and shuffled awkwardly toward shore.

He dropped the sack on the rough rocks. The metallic clink of gold coins hung in the air, a sound that should have signaled victory, but instead, it felt like a death knell. Escobar's smile, far from reassuring, sent ice through Lauren's veins.

"We can go?" she asked, her voice barely above a whisper.

Escobar's response extinguished the last flicker of hope she had left. "I let you go once before, and look at how that turned out. You just kept coming, didn't you?" His eyes, cold and remorseless, shifted to his waterlogged henchman. "That's what he's here for."

CHAPTER 39

A DESPERATE PLUNGE

Lauren and Ricardo stood frozen, their hearts pounding in their chests as they faced the hulking enforcer. His dead eyes bore into them, devoid of any emotion or mercy. The man's massive frame advanced, each step bringing them closer to their impending doom. Hope drained from their faces as they realized the gravity of their situation.

"But you have your gold," Lauren pleaded, her voice trembling with desperation.

Ricardo, grasping at straws, added, "My mother will never forgive you."

Escobar's lips curled into a cruel smile. He shrugged, dismissive of their pleas. "Nothing I can do."

The air was thick with tension, the sound of crashing waves a mocking reminder of the freedom just out of reach. Lauren's mind raced, searching for any escape, while Ricardo's eyes darted between Escobar, the enforcer, and the treacherously rocky shore.

Suddenly, the oppressive silence was shattered by the sound of splintering wood echoing from the house above. The unexpected noise drew the attention of their captors, their heads snapping towards the source of the commotion. Shouts in Portuguese filled the air, and figures emerged onto the back porch.

"Who dares?" Escobar exclaimed, his composure cracking for the first time.

In that split second of distraction, Lauren's survival instinct kicked in. With a surge of adrenaline, she pushed Ricardo towards the churning sea. "Now!" she hissed urgently.

Without hesitation, they dove into the crashing waves, disappearing beneath the surface. The shock of the cold water was nothing compared to the fear driving them forward. They kicked furiously, propelling themselves away from the shore, lungs burning as they fought to put as much distance as possible between themselves and certain death.

Lauren's heart raced as she swam, half-expecting to feel the impact of bullets piercing the surrounding water. She pushed herself to the limit, staying submerged until her lungs screamed for air. Breaking the surface, she gasped for air before diving again, letting the current carry her parallel to the shore.

On her second surfacing, Lauren frantically searched the shoreline. Relief washed over her as she noticed the trees obscured her view of Escobar's compound, meaning that she was hidden from view. The shouts from the shore were now indistinct, a cacophony of angry Portuguese voices carried on the wind.

Then, upon realizing that Ricardo was nowhere in sight, panic gripped her. She spun in the water, her eyes darting across the waves, praying for a sign of him. Seconds felt like hours as she bobbed in the sea, torn between the need to search for him and the fear of being spotted.

Just as despair set in, a head burst from the waves a few feet away. Ricardo emerged, spewing water and gasping for air, his face breaking into a broad smile as their eyes met.

Lauren kicked towards him, throwing her arms around his neck in a brief, desperate embrace. "I think we made it," she whispered, her voice a mix of exhaustion and cautious hope.

Ricardo nodded, his expression serious. "Maybe. But we need more distance. Can you swim to that public dock?" he asked, indicating a structure further down the shore.

Lauren nodded and summoned her last reserves of strength. "I think so."

"Stay underwater as much as possible," Ricardo instructed before taking a deep breath and disappearing beneath the surface himself. Lauren followed suit, her muscles protesting as she pushed herself to swim that last bit of distance.

The swim to the dock was grueling, requiring multiple breaks for air. By the time they approached the platform, Lauren was trembling with exhaustion and cold. Ricardo waited for her at the ladder. His own fatigue was carved into his features.

"Is it safe to get out?" Lauren asked, her teeth chattering.

Ricardo's eyes scanned the shoreline. "I hope so. But there's only one way to find out."

They climbed from the water with agonizing slowness, every muscle of theirs tensed for the sound of shouting or gunfire. Luckily, the only noise they heard was the lapping of waves and their own labored breathing. They had swum too far to hear the commotion at Escobar's compound.

As they made their way up the paved path to the road, relief mingled with their exhaustion. It was the same road that had brought them into Escobar's clutches.

Ricardo pointed in the direction opposite Escobar's lair. "Do you think the Global Runners are still swimming?"

Lauren's face brightened with hope. A small laugh escaped her lips. "God, I hope so. I could use a friendly face right about now."

Hand in hand, they began their trek back towards friends and safety, their wet clothes clinging to their bodies and the taste of salt covered their lips. Each step took them further from the nightmare they'd narrowly escaped. As they walked, the adrenaline wore off, only to be replaced by a bone-deep weariness and the realization of how close they had come to death. Lauren squeezed Ricardo's hand, grateful for his presence and their shared strength.

"We made it," she whispered, more to herself than to him.

Ricardo nodded, and his eyes were fixed on the road ahead. "We did. For now."

Lauren's steps faltered as the full weight of their situation hit her. They were alive, but Escobar was still here, and now, he had even more reason to come after them. Their ordeal was not yet over.

CHAPTER 40

THE BIGGEST MISTAKE

Duarte Escobar stood frozen, his eyes widening in disbelief as a swarm of police officers flooded his back porch. The sudden intrusion sent his mind reeling. He'd always prided himself on his connections, on the carefully cultivated network of corrupt officials who ensured that his business remained undisturbed. Yet, here they were, the very people he'd paid to look the other way, advancing on him with determined purpose.

A chill ran down his spine as he realized the gravity of the situation. The gun in his hand, moments ago a source of power, now represented his greatest threat. With a practiced flick of his wrist, he sent the pistol spinning through the air. It hit the water with a soft plop, quickly disappearing beneath the waves. Escobar allowed himself a moment of relief, but it was short-lived.

In his focus on the approaching officers and his own predicament, Escobar had forgotten about Carlos, his hulking enforcer. The man was more accustomed to using brute force than exercising judgment, and the sudden threat had triggered his instincts. Carlos hefted the long pipe he'd intended for Lauren and Ricardo, his dead eyes now fixed on the cluster of advancing policemen.

"*Parar!*" shouted the nearest officer, his hand moving toward his holster.

Escobar's head snapped around, suddenly aware of the danger. He opened his mouth to call Carlos off, but before he could utter a word, gunshots shattered the tense silence.

The pipe clattered to the rocky ground as Carlos staggered backward, his massive frame swaying like a felled tree. He looked down at his chest. Dark stains blossomed across his shirt, and he turned to Escobar with an expression of confusion. The light in his eyes dimmed as he crumpled to the ground, his fall seeming to happen in slow motion.

"*Espere!*" Escobar cried out, raising his hands higher in surrender, his heart pounding in his chest.

A lanky officer approached, his posture tense, but his voice measured. "*Senhor* Escobar, you can lower your hands. We see you are not armed." He paused, discomfort evident in his features. "It is very unusual for us to be this aggressive toward your home. For that, I apologize, but we have received orders from the Public Security ministry in Lisbon. They will arrive soon, along with representatives from the American Embassy."

Escobar's mind raced to search for a way out of this situation. He adopted a mask of innocent confusion. "Lieutenant, why would these offices be interested in my home? I'm just a local businessman."

The officer shifted uncomfortably, clearly torn between his duty and the unspoken arrangement that had long existed with Escobar. "Of course, we are aware of that. But we must collect from you certain national treasures that are in your possession." His gaze dropped pointedly to the sodden knapsack at Escobar's feet.

Escobar followed the officer's look and tried to construct a plausible explanation. "But we have just found that in the ocean, here at the edge of my property. How could word of this spread so quickly?"

Before the lieutenant could respond, a junior officer approached, struggling under the weight of a similar knapsack. "We found this one in the office closet," he reported, his voice tinged with a mix of excitement and apprehension.

The situation was spiraling out of control, but Escobar maintained his composure, his face a mask of benign bewilderment. Then, from across the yard, another officer's voice rang out, shattering any hope of salvaging the situation. "There's a body in this construction bag we found in the trunk of a car. Male. Single bullet hole to the chest."

The lieutenant's gaze hardened as he looked between Escobar and Carlos's crumpled form. "I seriously doubt that he ever owned a gun," he said, his voice now cold and professional. "*Senhor* Escobar, I must place you under arrest. We will hold you for the federal officers."

Desperation crept into Escobar's voice as he made one last attempt to regain control. "You are making a big mistake, Lieutenant. You might reconsider this."

The officer's response was resolute. "*Senhor*, if the man in the bag is American, it is you who has made the mistake. We cannot protect you from them."

As his new reality sank in, Escobar watched in stunned silence as the police officers methodically swept through his property. They moved with a purpose that spoke of thorough preparation, collecting evidence with practiced efficiency. Victor's body, still bearing his American

passport, was easily identified and removed. The gold from both bags, quickly identified as priceless artifacts from Portugal's storied past, was cataloged and secured.

Escobar was led to a waiting police car, the weight of handcuffs on his wrists a stark reminder of how quickly his empire could crumble. As he was driven away, he caught a last glimpse of his once-impregnable sanctuary, now swarming with law enforcement.

In the chaos of the raid, with its rich haul of evidence and the shock of discovering a body, no one thought to search the surrounding waters for additional victims or accomplices. The police remained unaware that their timely arrival had prevented two more gruesome deaths.

CHAPTER 41

EMOTIONAL EXHAUSTION

Ricardo and Lauren returned to the runners' swimming party. The afternoon sun that warmed everyone else seemed to provide no heat to their chilled bodies. Their footsteps were unsteady as they approached the group, leaving wet footprints in their wake.

Sheryl's sharp intake of breath cut through the cheerful chatter of the runners. "Oh, my God! What happened to you two?" Her usually composed demeanor cracked at the sight of their pale faces and haunted expressions. "Are you okay? Do you need medical help?" Without waiting for a response, she spun around, her voice taking on an urgent edge. "Isabella, I think we need your help!"

The pair collapsed onto the ground, their legs finally giving out. Lauren's voice came out as barely more than a whisper. "We…had some trouble." The words felt inadequate, almost absurd in their simplicity.

Ricardo shook his head slowly, his usually animated face drawn and tired. "I think we'll be okay. Just exhausted…and cold." His voice carried a weight that suggested much more than physical fatigue.

The group mobilized quickly around them. Sheryl and Isabella wrapped them in thick towels, their practiced movements suggesting they'd handled their share of emergencies. Soon, the pair found themselves on the bus, wearing borrowed clothes that felt oddly normal against their still-trembling skin. They devoured the food brought to them, their bodies demanding sustenance, even as their minds struggled to process the events of the past few hours.

The curious faces of their fellow runners appeared at the bus windows, but neither Lauren, nor Ricardo could find the words to explain. Eventually, they just gave up and sat in silence, staring straight ahead, the weight of their experience hanging heavy between them.

"I don't understand how we're even alive," Lauren finally said in a voice that was barely above a whisper.

Ricardo's response carried the echo of his deeply held faith. "Divine intervention. A bigger purpose." His eyes held a distant look, as if seeing beyond the physical world to something greater.

"Something in the universe helped us. We didn't do that on our own," Lauren agreed, finding comfort in the thought of forces bigger than themselves.

Ricardo turned to her suddenly, realization dawning on his face. "You did it. You pushed us into the sea. If you hadn't, we would have been shot, beaten, or arrested. But here we are, free and safe." His words carried both gratitude and amazement.

A gentle knock interrupted their moment. "Knock, knock." John's weathered face appeared at the bus door. "Can I come in?"

"Sure, John. You, at least, understand some of the story."

John's next word fell like a stone into still water: "Escobar?"

The name sent visible tremors through both of them, and tears welled in Lauren's eyes. "He was going to kill us," she managed before falling silent, the words seeming to drain what little energy she had left.

With John as their witness, Ricardo and Lauren gradually pieced together their story, each taking turns to fill in the gaps the other couldn't bear to voice. The retelling seemed to release some of the terror that had gripped them, like lancing a wound to let it heal.

John listened intently, his face growing grave. When they finished, he sat in contemplative silence before sharing his own role in their salvation.

"You remember telling us about retrieving the gold from Escobar's home? Well, when I realized that the treasure would be easy for the authorities to find, I called the Ministry of the Interior in Lisbon. I was passed through several bureaucrats before I arrived at someone who was interested in important historical artifacts. Then, it took some time to convince her I wasn't a crackpot."

Lauren and Ricardo were listening in astonishment. Lauren said, "How did you get them to believe you?"

"I got her cell number and sent a text with a picture of the coins we had. That got her attention immediately. Then, I explained where all the coins were and who had them. She seemed to grasp the importance of that immediately. She just said, 'We'll take care of it,' and hung up."

"So, the people who raided Escobar's house were feds from the mainland?" Lauren asked.

"I don't know. Maybe." John shrugged, surprised that the government would act so fast on such a random call.

At that moment, a familiar face appeared at the front of the bus. "Lauren, could I talk to you?" Stacy's voice

was nervous and weak. Her appearance brought a new tension to the air.

Lauren's eyes narrowed, remembering her discovery on the kayak. "Stacy, I can't handle more backstabbing right now."

Stacy's face went white. "Then you know? Well, that's what I wanted to tell you."

"That you've been reporting my activities to Escobar?" Lauren said bitterly. Ricardo's head shot up, and he stood to protect Lauren from this new threat.

"Initially, yes. But there's more you need to know." Stacy waited for permission to continue. "Victor hired me. You know how charming he can be. He said he just wanted to make sure you were alright. But then, he introduced me to Escobar, and I knew it was a lot more than that. It had to be something worth a lot of money. You can just feel the evil oozing off that man." She shivered at memories of their first meeting.

"Go on," Lauren prompted.

"Well, I would tell Victor where you went or what we were doing every day." Stacy's voice caught in her throat. "Anyway, yesterday, we were talking on the phone when I heard shouting in the background. It was Escobar going on about betrayal. Victor sounded afraid. There was a gunshot, and the line went dead. I called the local police and told them that Escobar had killed Victor and he was an American. I didn't believe it fully, but I knew it would get their attention at the very least."

Lauren said, "It's true. Escobar told us he killed Victor. And he was going to do the same to us."

When Stacy learned of Victor's fate, her face turned white as she realized she could have been caught in the same trap.

As the sun cast long shadows through the bus windows, they all waited in collective exhaustion; it was emotionally, physically, and spiritually draining. The realization that their survival hinged on the actions of both John and Stacy, two unlikely guardian angels, left Ricardo and Lauren in a state of stunned gratitude.

The bus had become a confessional of sorts, where truth and tears flowed freely, where the boundaries between friend and foe blurred, and where the full weight of their brush with death could finally be acknowledged.

CHAPTER 42

A TOAST

The hotel banquet room glowed with warm light from ornate chandeliers, their crystals casting abstract patterns across the walls. The space hummed with laughter and animated conversation as the Global Runners filtered in for their farewell dinner. Servers in white shirts circulated with trays of the local wine, the golden liquid catching the light like liquid sunshine.

The room had been transformed for the occasion. White tablecloths draped round tables adorned with centerpieces of native Azorean flowers: hydrangeas in deep blues and purples mixed with delicate white orchids. Through the tall windows, the setting sun painted the sky in spectacular shades of orange and pink, framing the looming silhouette of Pico's massive volcano. It was a fitting backdrop for their final gathering.

Sheryl, resplendent in a flowing summer dress, raised her glass high. Her voice carried across the room with the authority of a seasoned tour leader. "A toast to good times, good friends, and good runs!"

The sound of clinking glasses filled the air like musical chimes, followed by appreciative murmurs as the runners enjoyed the crisp, fruity wine. The mood was festive, with everyone sharing stories and laughter, recounting their favorite moments from the week's adventures.

Lauren and Ricardo had joined the celebration, despite their ordeal, drawn by their need for safe camaraderie. They found themselves in a corner with John and Sandra, creating their own intimate circle of shared experiences. The wine helped ease their lingering tension. It brought color back to their cheeks and smiles to their faces.

Sandra, her eyes twinkling with mischief, produced her Sebastian gold coin after her second glass of wine. "We may not be rich, but we have these. I'll try to remember the excitement of the search for and discovery of this treasure, not the terror that followed." The others

followed suit, their coins catching the light as they clinked them together in a secret toast. The gesture felt like a completion of their shared adventure, a way to reclaim the excitement of discovery from the shadow of danger.

Stacy approached Lauren, her face softening with genuine remorse. "Again, I'm so sorry for the trouble I caused you. But I did get the police to come to your rescue just in time."

Lauren's response carried a newfound warmth. "You did. They may have responded less urgently if they had not heard from both you and John. For that, I am grateful to you and the universe."

The room filled with the aroma of local delicacies as servers brought out platters of fresh seafood, grilled meats, and traditional Azorean dishes. Sheryl, who had been watching her guests with the pride of a mother hen, made her way through the increasingly boisterous crowd to Lauren and Ricardo.

She realized her guests had been through much more than just a running vacation, but she had little inkling of the depths of the nightmare they'd endured. Placing an arm around Lauren's shoulders and a hand on Ricardo's, she fixed them with her signature sparkling smile. "This week has been more exhausting for you than we expected. But I hope we were able to give you a vacation worth remembering all the same."

Then, turning to Ricardo, she said, "And I've noticed that you played a major role in caring for this little group. So, I want to show my appreciation by making you an honorary member of the Global Runners' staff." She extended a hand with a small plastic button in it. Pinching Ricardo's shirt, she snapped it closed on his collar. "With this GR bib board, I appoint you GR staff. Next time we come to the islands, I want you to work for us officially…with pay."

Ricardo chuckled at the ceremonial invitation. "I accept. Just call me, and I'll be there."

Sheryl turned to Lauren next. "We're all leaving tomorrow. I suspect that will be harder for you than the rest of us." She tipped her head toward Ricardo.

Lauren nodded in agreement. "It would be…if I were leaving. But I've decided to stay for a while. There's so much more to see and do that I've missed out on."

This announcement was news to everyone, including Ricardo, who broke into an enormous smile.

"Good for you," Sheryl said.

John raised his glass once more, his voice carrying the weight of someone who knew the full story of what had occurred. "A toast. To new adventures and new friendships. May they be safe and prosperous."

As the formal dinner concluded, the energy in the room shifted into full celebration mode. Someone

dimmed the chandeliers and set up colored spotlights. A disco ball appeared as if by magic, sending sparkles of light spinning across the room like stars. The music system came alive with the pulsing beats of both American and Portuguese hits.

The runners, many of whom had shown remarkable endurance on the trails, now showed equally impressive stamina on the dance floor. They moved as one when their unofficial anthem played, their voices joining in a joyous chorus of Raffaella Carrà's "Pedro, Pedro, Pedro!" The song had become their rally cry during the week.

Couples spun and swayed, groups formed impromptu conga lines, and even the most reserved runners found themselves swept up in the celebration. Lauren and Ricardo joined the dancing, their earlier exhaustion forgotten in the euphoria of the moment. Their movements together spoke of a future filled with promise, their shared smiles reflecting the joy of new beginnings.

The party continued late into the night, a perfect blend of a farewell celebration and a promise of new beginnings. Through the windows, the stars above the Azores twinkled their approval, silent witnesses to the end of one adventure and the beginning of another.

CHAPTER 43

PERMISSION

John and Sandra navigated the labyrinthine streets of Lisbon, where their extraordinary adventure had begun just days ago. Despite their previous visit, the Alfama quarter seemed determined to guard its secrets, with narrow cobblestone streets twisting and turning. The afternoon sun cast long shadows across weathered buildings, making familiar landmarks appear mysteriously different.

After several wrong turns and dead ends, they finally emerged onto the small street housing Emilio's antiquities shop. The battered sign above the door creaked gently in the breeze, its gold lettering barely visible against the aged wood. This time, they approached not as curious tourists, but as people returning home from a profound journey.

Inside, time seemed to have been frozen, awaiting their return. The small, leathery man sat in his familiar position, bent over his workbench with the concentration of an artist. His skilled hands moved deliberately over another brass object, his fingers dancing across its surface with the expertise gained by a lifetime of work.

"*Bom dia, Senhor* Emilio. We have returned from our quest." John's voice carried warmth and respect.

The owner's wrinkled face creased into a gentle smile. "*Bem-vindo à minha cidade das maravilhas.*" The familiar greeting to the city of wonders resonated differently now.

John proudly delivered his practiced Portuguese: "*Encontramos o tesouro,*" informing the man that they had found the treasure they searched for.

Emilio's serene response and subsequent conversation revealed depths to his character they hadn't suspected during their first visit. Emilio replied, "Yes, I know. Among antiquity dealers, the news has spread around the world. Congratulations. Was the adventure everything you hoped it would be?"

"Actually, it was more terrifying than we expected." As John recounted their adventure, the old man listened with the patience of someone who had heard many such tales over the years, yet remained fascinated with each one. John ended with the treasure in the hands of the Ministry of the Interior.

Emilio nodded. "That is where it belongs." Then, he added, "But you have a small souvenir for yourself?"

"Yes, we do. A few coins to remember the adventure and the history that inspired it."

"I think King Sebastian would approve. You may take it with you. May it bring you the same luck and protection that it has given to my family for generations." The shop itself seemed to grow quieter, as if the very artifacts were listening to this passing of historical legacy.

In granting them permission to keep their coins, Emilio's words carried the gravity of royal proclamation. For the first time, John wondered if this man was more than just a small shop owner. *Can his family trace its origins to King Sebastian himself? Is it possible that he spoke for the royal family in releasing the coins to an American couple?*

"We appreciate the guidance you gave us. We won't forget you, *Senhor* Emilio, 1972." Glancing up at the wooden plaque of owners, he noticed a new name had been added, "Pedro, 2024." John asked, "You are passing the shop to your son?"

"Si. It was my job to reveal Sebastian's treasure. You and your friends have done that for me. Now, it is time for someone new to care for these treasures." Emilio exhaled, and a visible burden seemed to lift from his shoulders.

Emilio's admission that his task was complete added profound meaning to the couple's adventure. They had helped fulfill a mission that was generations in the making. Sandra laid a soft hand on Emilio's leathery arm. "Our gratitude goes with you." Her simple statement encompassed not just their adventure, but an appreciation for the preservation of history.

"*Bom dia.*" With that, the old man stood and walked feebly into the deep shadows of the shop.

John and Sandra stood for a moment, absorbing the atmosphere. The shop had been their gateway to an incredible adventure, and now, it served as the epilogue to their tale. They stepped back into the sunshine of modern Lisbon, carrying with them not just a gold coin, but a connection to centuries of Portuguese history and the memory of a mysterious shopkeeper who had guided their Azorean adventure.

CHAPTER 44

RETURNING

"*Querida*, do you have your water?" Ricardo asked, his voice carrying a tenderness that had grown stronger with each passing day.

"Yes, *coracao*." Lauren smiled at their exchange of endearments. She knew only a few simple terms in Portuguese, but these had become precious to her, like secret words shared between high school sweethearts. "Do you have the headlamps?"

After double checking their gear with the comfortable rhythm of experienced hiking partners, they began their trek up the familiar trail. The morning sun painted the landscape in gentle golds and greens, so different from the tension-filled atmosphere of their previous ascent.

"It's a beautiful morning. No fog," Ricardo said, reaching for her hand as they walked.

"I'm enjoying these views of Pico's volcano more than we did the first time." Though Lauren knew they were safe, she caught herself glancing down the approaching road as they entered the wooded area. The memory of that green pickup still lurked in the shadows of her mind.

"He's in jail," Ricardo assured her and squeezed her hand. His voice carried the quiet confidence that had become her anchor. "No one will bother us. I've climbed this mountain dozens of times and never ran into trouble...except that one time."

Lauren thought, *I wish we could say the same for Victor. He might have been a bastard to me, but he didn't deserve to be killed for choosing the wrong business partner.* To Ricardo, she said, "I trust you. It's going to be a magical day. So, the plan is to hike all the way to the top this time?"

"Right. I want you to see how beautiful the island is from up there." Ricardo's eyes sparkled with pride for his homeland. "If it remains clear like this, we'll be able to see four islands—Faial, São Jorge, Graciosa, and Terceira. Most people come and go from the Azores without ever getting this grand view."

As they climbed, Lauren noticed how light her pack felt—as well as her heart. The weight of their ordeal with Duarte Escobar had lifted gradually over the past week, replaced by something warmer, something that made her pulse quicken when Ricardo looked her way. The legal complications and financial arrangements had been sorted out, leaving them free to focus on what was growing between them.

"With a stop at our favorite place," Lauren added, a hint of adventure returning to her voice.

"Yes, with a stop," Ricardo agreed. His tone suggested that he'd follow her anywhere.

The fork in the path appeared sooner than expected. They paused at the crossroad, but this time, instead of feeling ghostly tendrils of fear, Lauren felt only the thrill of shared memories. The left branch beckoned them toward the Costa ranch house and its hidden tunnel.

Sitting on the ruined wall of the house, Lauren took a long drink from her bottle. The valley spread before them like a painting, the emerald fields cascading toward the distant ocean. "This view is much better than the one we had last time. I can see why Captain Costa would choose this spot for his home."

Ricardo sat close to settle his arm around her shoulders. His deep, relaxed breath carried the contentment of a man exactly where he wanted to be. "Shall we clamber through those trees to the lava tunnel entrance?"

"I'm ready." Lauren shouldered her pack and strapped the headlamp to her forehead, feeling none of the trepidation that had marked their previous descent.

The tunnel entrance greeted them like an old friend. Inside, their headlamps cut through the darkness with confident beams. Lauren looked left. "It's up there," she said, her voice carrying both nostalgia and excitement for what they might find.

They made their way to the sacred spot where their lives had changed forever. The abandoned gear lay scattered exactly as they'd left it, a testament that the tunnel's secrets had remained undisturbed in their absence.

"That's a good sign," Ricardo said. "If our gear is still here, then no one else has been here."

The adventurers turned their attention to the crumbled remains of the ancient chest. Lauren extracted her shovel and cleared away debris. She moved the formless fibers that had once been wooden planks. Hidden within it were fragments of rusted and decayed iron bands and hinges.

As she expected, she saw the golden reflection of treasure left behind. "I knew we left some coins buried in this mess, but they had seemed unimportant at the time. We had so much more in those backpacks."

With the tip of the shovel, she lifted out one coin and then another. Ricardo plucked each from the debris, dropping them into a small sack.

"How many do we have now?" Lauren asked, her archaeologist's instincts fully engaged.

"Four. Keep digging," Ricardo urged, his excitement matching hers.

"Seven coins," Ricardo announced finally. "That's good. It's the number of perfection and completeness."

Frowning, Lauren said, "I thought there'd be more. It just seemed deeper the last time we were here." Determined not to miss any this time, Lauren scraped the shovel back and forth across the underlying rocks. One large rock tipped up on the edge of the shovel. She reached down and flipped it over. It was wide, smooth, and almost rectangular. Something about it triggered a memory. "Shine your light here."

Under their combined beams, a chiseled diagram emerged from centuries of darkness. A rust stain traced one edge where an iron band had once been mounted. "Do you know what this is?" she asked.

"Maybe someone's name?" Ricardo ventured.

"It's a map," Lauren declared, her voice carrying the thrill of discovery.

"To what?" Ricardo asked while leaning closer.

Lauren was silent for several moments, savoring the implications of what lay before them. When she finally spoke, her voice quavered with excitement. "There's another gold chest hidden on this island."

Ricardo's eyes went wide at the suggestion, and in them, Lauren saw the same spark of excitement that had first drawn them together. Whatever lay ahead, they would discover it together.

THE END

BONUS: LAUREN BANISTER, FIELD WORK

Join our newsletter community to receive an exclusive bonus story following Lauren Banister's search for antiquities.

https://www.rddsmith.com/laurenbanister

Also check out the Medical Thrillers by R.D.D. Smith

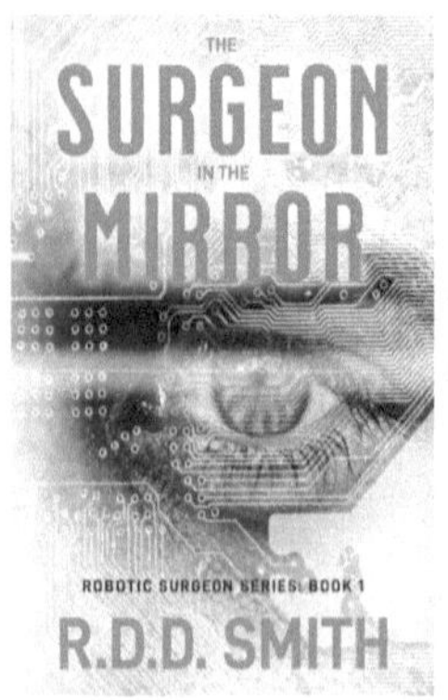

https://www.rddsmith.com/books

or

https://www.amazon.com/dp/B0C59ZRZDR

AI DISCLOSURE

The text of this novel was written by the human author. I used GPT-4 and Claude as research tools to collect cultural, historical, geographical, and geological information on Portugal and the Azores Islands.

ABOUT R.D.D. SMITH

Dr. Roger Smith writes (1) science-fiction, medical thriller novels featuring advanced surgical devices, AI, telesurgery, simulation, and speculative diseases, and (2) travel adventures that follow a group of running tourists through exotic countries. The medical series is inspired by his career in healthcare and experience with robotic surgery devices. The travel novels are inspired by his actual vacations in the countries featured in the books.

Prior to writing fiction, he enjoyed a goldilocks career in healthcare, government, and national defense. For ten years, he was a leading robotic surgery researcher, publishing his results in medical journals and speaking at surgical conferences. He spent four years in civilian government service, leading the technology innovation for all U.S. Army simulation systems. Prior to that, he was a vice president for multiple defense software companies.

Dr. Smith has received multiple awards for his innovations in robotic surgery education, training simulation, and software system development. He is on the faculty of the University of Central Florida's College of Medicine and the Institute for Simulation and Training.

He holds a doctorate and MBA from the University of Maryland, a master's from Texas Tech University, and a bachelor's from Colorado State University.

He lives with his wife, dogs, and cats in sunny Florida, frequently escaping to cooler climes during the beastly Florida summers.

STAY IN TOUCH

Review:
Please leave a review of this book on Amazon or your favorite book site.

Join Us:
Join our community of readers to receive fascinating news related to the story.

www.rddsmith.com/free

ACKNOWLEDGMENTS

As an author, I am infinitely grateful to my readers who invest their time, money, and imaginations in following my stories and characters through their challenges, failures, and transformations.

First, to my wife and children, who have endured decades of fanatic immersion into whatever my latest passion is, most recently, these novels. Your patience, dedication, and love are appreciated every day.

For this adventure story, I am indebted to Vacation Races Global Adventures (USA) and Our Island (Azores) for organizing the fantastic trip that inspired the events in this novel. Special thanks to Cheri Santiego, Zoe Calcott, and Salem Stanley for creating a business, an adventure, a community, and a family all in one. Thank you to my fellow vacationers and runners for your enthusiastic encouragement as we created and discovered each chapter of this book together.

For my editor Kaitlin Travis, book layout artist Adina Cucicov, and the many advisors who made this book far better than I could have accomplished alone.

If you're looking for running adventure travel:

Vacation Races Global Adventures
https://www.vacationraces.com/global-adventures/

Our Island Azores
https://ourisland-azores.com/

Photo Credit: Juliana Costa, Used with Permission